The Man With

And Other Strange, Terrifying Tales

By

Graham Anthony-Thomas

10 9 8 7 6 5 4 3 2 1

Contents

Author's Note

When putting this anthology of strange tales together I was reminded of the stories I used to read as a kid from some of the great horror and mystery writers of the day. People like Robert Bloch, Ray Bradbury, Stephen King, Dean Koontz and Alistair MacLean.

As a younger person, I spent hours poring over their books and wondering about the darker, more sinister side of life, sometimes filled with high adventure, sometimes filled with fear. And as my friends used to play out and do the things other young men did, my mind wandered in less trod corridors inside, which, in turn, fuelled my imagination and hence the anthology you are about to read.

The stories I present here were written many years ago and, yes, I have tinkered here and there, but by-and-large they are true to their original content and I'm very pleased with their perspective. Personal favourite? I'm not sure, 'The Man With No Face', is one I still have a strong attachment to, even though it was written 20 years ago. Doesn't time fly? And the time has come – 'the Walrus said' – to release these stories that mean so much to me.

So here, take it. Read it. Think about it. I give you my first collection of strange mysteries. After so many years of writing non-fiction this, my first published work of fiction, I give to you to enjoy with nervous excitement; well, I hope so anyway. Do you feel the tingle of anticipation, dear reader? Maybe a tinge of dread? It is interesting that these stories are mysteries to some, plottings to others and, why so many road accidents, I don't know; but I do hope you enjoy them, I really do. I hope that you read these stories over and over and that they entertain you. They may even inspire you. As a stage director, I'm on the look-out for more incredible stories... be warned. Adieu!

Graham Anthony-Thomas
Warminster, August 2014

George

George swivelled away from the little porthole, his only window to the vast, loneliness of space and wondered how long it would take to die. Rolling down the narrow corridor of the cramped ship, his wheels squeaking and groaning over the metal floor, this thought kept reverberating in his mind.

How long, he thought, before everything just ran down to silence? No life support, no reactors, no computers just silently drifting in space. How long?

Rolling towards the communications room was a task he had done millions of times since they launched and would do millions of times until the ship finally lost its power. How long ago did they blast into this frozen space?

Once in the communications room, his eyes travelled over the instruments, digital read-outs, LED screens and monitors. They were so old now that each calculation was a little slower than the one before as their output dropped slowly with the last reactor's gradual descent into silence.

Only sixty percent power remained. George had to close Battery Rooms 4 and 7 because of leakage. The casing had become brittle and cracked with age, spilling their acid onto the metal floor. George knew the acid was slowly eating through the steel bulkheads and may get to the hull. And after all what did it matter.

Everyday he went slowly through the ship shutting down another system that they could do without. Most of the ship's sensor array lay dormant waiting for a signal or a sign.

Everything was a slow, plodding, steady decline to the final shut-down when he would be helpless, without power, without light, just drifting uselessly in space, light years away from his home.

Home.

What was that like now, he wondered? What was home? The laboratory? It had been a maze of buildings and labs with rows of laptop computers and electrical parts, with the vats where the cells were cloned, with the giant robotics section. What, he wondered, would it be like now?

Wasn't home on an island somewhere surrounded by blue sea?

He couldn't remember. It was all somewhere on the computer but he was too tired and too bored to look for it.

Suddenly, the faint sound of metal wheels screeching on metal drifted into communications. George twisted his face into a smile as the noise grew louder. A moment later his companion Lucy trundled through the doorway and his smile turned into a frown.

"Lucy! What have you been doing?" His loud, high-pitched wail echoed through the metal room.

"I have been putting on my face. Do you like it?"

"No!" He rolled over to her, watching her preen at her reflection on the largest LED screen, once their main navigation computer but now a worn-out piece of useless hardware.

Holding her hands to her face she was trying to smooth a grey, flaking, material to the contours of her cheeks. "Don't you think it makes me look younger? Almost alive?"

"No, I don't!" He cried as he grabbed her hand, pulling the material from her face. "You can't keep skinning the humans! I've told you before."

"But they're frozen. They don't feel anything!"

"Lucy, the humans are dead and have been for years. This is dead skin! Look at it, as soon as it leaves cryogenics it turns to dust."

Her eyes travelled to the skin crumbling in his hands. "You see," he whispered, "just dust."

"But it's not true. It will make me young, make me be a human too, like we used to be."

Slowly, pulling her away from the screen he lead her across the room to a working console. "You have to face it, Lucy. Our skin and flesh has long since rotted away. They made us into machines."

"Why?"

For a moment, George stared at Lucy's large, humanoid eyes. Eyes that were deeply blue and very beautiful but artificial, made of fibre optics and soft, permanent lenses that never failed.

Thinking about her question he realised he had no answers.

"I don't know, Lucy." Why did they turn them into machines? He couldn't be sure. He glanced at her and shrugged. "For prolonged space travel, I guess. Anyway the point is our skin is long gone. Look at me. I'm metal now, my flesh and skin gone. I don't complain and neither should you."

"But I want to be human."

"Yes, I know. You can't be but you can enjoy the next best thing. " He saw the anticipation in her eyes and turned to the console pulling a small headset from it.

"Shall we have Gone With The Wind, again, my dear?"

"Oh, yes, yes," she cried excitedly as he put the headset over her metallic head and pulled a visor in front of her eyes.

Within seconds he saw images appear on the visor, felt a wave of relief flood over him knowing she would be absorbed in the story for hours giving him time to be on his own. Over the years her power cells had slowly faded turning her into a child.

He worried that soon his own power cells would slowly die and he would lose his ability to reason, to think clearly. Since launch he had been through every memory bank, every chip, every circuit and sucked out all the information the computer had. For their benefit, every book ever written had been programmed into the memory banks of the ship's computers, so they would never get bored, never be at a loss for what to do. There would always be a good book. Now, he no longer cared and Lucy had stopped caring long before he did.

For decades or was it centuries he merely did the tasks assigned to him from the beginning and would until the power stopped flowing and became like Lucy, aimless and uncaring. Instead of enjoying the classics, an anthology of short stories, a gripping novel or terror, he stared out the little porthole at the inky blackness outside and the millions of twinkling stars.

Though it seemed like the ship was crawling, he knew they were hurtling through space, gaining momentum and speed each day. The occasional burst of the old retro-rockets merely served to increase their velocity.

The Makers were right, he thought as he rolled sideways over the floor in front of the control panel. The further away you get the faster you go and the more time slows down. A minute to me would be a month or a year to everybody back home. All the instruments registered normal, all systems functioning at 60%, no sign of life, planets, ships, asteroids or anything for hundreds of miles in all directions. It had been this way for decades.

That was what made it so tedious. Their task had been to listen and search for intelligent, extraterrestrial life using powerful radio telescopes and sensor arrays.

Years ago the telescope had been destroyed by an asteroid shower and the sensors had lost so much power they were unreliable if left on for prolonged periods. So George turned them on for only an hour or two each day, defeating their intended programming.

I haven't aged, thought George. I'm still the same as I was.

He knew he had never been designed to age because George was 70% machine and the rest human. He was a servo-byoid, one of the first of his kind. Designed specifically for space travel, he never aged, didn't have legs but had a metal skeleton with a bio-electronic functioning heart and brain. His heart pumped a brownish reddish liquid through his veins, that acted as blood, collecting oxygen for the few living cells the liquid carried, sending it to the plexal seals and joints, as a lubricant, intertwined with his metal skeleton.

But from the waist down, George was a metal chair, a stump full of circuits and chips on four wheels, connected to the ship's computer by a receiving chip in his head so, no mater where he was, he would always know the condition of the ship instantly.

Long ago, as the skin died on his face and hands leaving patches of bare metal he looked ugly and devilish. Since Lucy had gone senile she never remarked on his grotesque appearance so he didn't care if he let himself go. It just didn't matter.

The noisy metal wheels of his chair squeaked as he rolled down the curving corridor of the ship. A door hissed open as he entered the Cryogenics section. In front of him were eight glass tubes arrayed in a circle with the cryogenic computers as the core around which they were placed like spokes on a wheel.

Of the eight chambers, five were open, their glass canopies cracked and erect reaching up to the ceiling. He rolled to the nearest one, peering inside. The smell had long since gone. Now, all that remained of the human was the skeleton crumbling into dust, layers of skin hanging from the bone where Lucy had long ago sliced most of it away. He looked at the grey bones, and the grey powder they lay in. A slight shudder ran through him as he turned away and he suddenly wondered if he was more human than he thought.

Slowly, he rolled on to each of the open cryogenic chambers where in each one he saw a similar sight. Of the last three, two were also dead. In each of these, the

12

canopies had cracked and split contaminating the chamber with outside air and causing the process to malfunction. The occupants had died quickly, suddenly ageing and, thankfully, never returning to consciousness.

He stopped at the one chamber still active and stared down at the young woman lying naked inside. She was very pretty, he thought.

"If I was a real man....." He let the thought drift away.

For sometime he had been toying with tampering with the program for her chamber to make sure she would never recover. Each time his finger hovered over the large red button just below the canopy he found he could not push it knowing the change in pressure, temperature and air would kill her.

What would she wake up to? He shook his head. "What is there for you here? Two half demented robots on a dying ship."

All her companions were dead. If she did wake up she would wake up to nothing. Not a living soul for hundreds of light years in all directions. No one to talk to, no one to be with. "Just emptiness in the vastness of space, my dear. I think it's time we said good-bye. You'll be better off, believe me."

Staring at her smooth, calm face, he knew she couldn't hear him but it didn't mater. His finger hovered over the button. Suddenly, he remembered their objective. What if they do pick-up something? The system was designed to bring the humans out of consciousness once the sensors picked up life forms. If that did happen she would have to deal with that as well. Should I, or shouldn't I, he thought? He stared at the red button, then let his eyes wander over the young woman's body for several minutes. "I'll wait till tomorrow to decide. You've got a day's reprieve my dear."

Turning suddenly, George rolled quickly out of the cryogenics room into the winding corridor leaving the warning behind him as the doors quickly closed. He chuckled to himself. Everyday he went through the same routine and each time it took longer for him to tell her she had a reprieve.

One day he would press the button. One day soon. But he had to admit she did have lovely features. His only concern was keeping Lucy away from her.

Like a saucer, with a long tail, their ship, home for their entire existence was cramped and noisy. There were no creature comforts because his creators didn't think they needed them. Except for one room. George knew there was a room for the humans off the cryogenics chamber for them to use when they woke. It was supposed to be fully stocked and comfortable but he didn't know because he had never been inside. It was the only room that his receiver did not work in, which meant he could not enter it without completely shutting down.

The Makers didn't think robots needed creature comforts. No, of course not, he thought bitterly. Robots don't need sleep, or take delight in eating a hot meal, or listening to great music, or speak from imperfect lips or feel the stabbing pain of loneliness,or sit on a soft chair, or lie in a fluffy bed, or feel delicate material against their faces.

They were wrong.

All the important books in the world, he brooded, and they couldn't give me the decency of real movement. He had read everything they gave him and his bio-fibronic MS 600 multiple impulse brain took it all in, building on his original programming enabling him to surpass all his parameters and virtually recreate himself.

True, he thought, at lift-off so long ago, he and Lucy were just robots permanently mated to the onboard computers but their makers had programmed every important book, from science to love, in the memory banks and now he could think and feel beyond what the Makers had ever planned.

George understood loneliness.

He had for decades since Lucy had gone senile and the computers had slowed down so much he couldn't interface with them. They were like witless, gibbering, fools compared with him. In the early days, as they tore passed Saturn, Jupiter to Pluto and beyond George and the ship's central computer system argued endlessly on logic, mathematics, physics theories of space and time, Newtonian laws of gravity, bone structure, the list went on and on. He and Lucy had taken those arguments and extrapolated far beyond the ship's systems.

Those days were gone. He remembered how stronger they became with every book they read, every theory they understood and evaluated. Gradually, their arguments against the all powerful ship's network grew stronger and stronger, until the day came when they could both out calculate and out think them in every area. When that day happened both he and Lucy felt a strong surge of triumph! Since then, Lucy had just shut down and stopped caring. There had been no goal, no cause to think about, no life spark to keep them active after beating the main onboard computers.

All systems functioning.

The great solar reactors for the onboards, arranged in long rows of the ships spine, behind the cramped, tiny saucer were still running, still creating energy. Running at just over half their original capacity George prided himself on how efficient he'd made them. Rolling by the shining cylinders, their cooling trunks coiled around their smooth casings like a forest of tentacles, he could hear the humming, the vibrating as the old generators pumped out

16

the power. Everyday, they sounded just a little rougher.

The door at the end of the power room slid open as he rolled on, leaving the large reactors behind him. The chair squeaked and bounced over the metal surface of what was a combination auxiliary control and observation room. The chair moved quickly around large computer servers, storage cabinets, radar receivers and transmitters, sensor arrays, solar transformers, water and heat pumps, towards the very end of the room which was also the end of the ship, at the very tip of its long spine.

Here, three large portholes gave George the only view of the empty, vast, space he was floating in. Behind him, along the back wall LED monitors slowly scrolled out a ragged flow of information on all the ships systems, including some of his own.

Soon, he knew they would reach the final co-ordinates where they were to circle and float for eternity. The furthest outpost of a new regime called the Triunal. The signal telling him to hold his position came several months ago.

What was the Triunal? Just another way for humans to destroy themselves, he thought.

Yes, he would hold his position, but he didn't see what good it would do. Nobody else was out this far.

Suddenly, the screens stopped their usual flood of

information. Somewhere on the ship the warning klaxon sounded.

Swivelling, he stared at the screens.

UNIDENTIFIED SIGNAL RECEIVED.

The words flashed across the screens, as the klaxon wailed. It couldn't be.

He knew the drill. The onboards wouldn't be going this crazy, he thought, unless they'd picked up a signal. Turning back to his porthole he stared into the black emptiness. Something, or someone else was out there. That means, he thought, the human would be waking up as he stood there. Damn It! Now report after report would have to be made to the human. Check after check. The systems would have to be overhauled again and again to verify the signal was indeed a signal and not a system malfunction.

The screens were going crazy pouring out data.

Suddenly the ship shuddered violently. The retros at the back, underneath him were firing, slowing the ship to a snail's pace as the computers monitored the signal. So much work to do, he sighed. But the first thing he knew he had to do was greet the human.

Turning quickly, he rolled away towards the cryogenic chamber, hoping she wouldn't die of fright.

Harrington's Gone

It was the crows that made the place so eerie. They never stopped crying. Hundreds of crows cawing in the four highest trees. The trees themselves, ancient, tall, with no branches on the trunk except at the very top, seemed strange, eerie and mystical in the crawling mist. The crows had nested in the thick vegetation at the top of these trees that swayed in the low moaning wind. Though it was July it felt like October. Dreary, damp, overcast and unearthly.

"I'm not going down there!" Helen whispered.

Burton slammed the car door and locked it. "We have no choice," he said flatly. He glanced at the others all standing by the car looking around the deserted car park. "Let's go."

"Wait!" Stevens turned his massive frame towards the trees, pointing. "It looks like we're not alone."

Looking in the same direction, Burton saw a car parked at the far end, under a low willow tree, almost totally obscured by the branches. "It's Harrington's." They ran towards it.

All four looked at the deserted Audi that Harrington had used to get to this strange, dark, remote place, just outside Helford in Cornwall.

"It's his, alright." Burton said, peering inside the car. He saw nothing out of the ordinary but checked the door.

To his surprise it opened. "Well, well," he said in the way a story-book detective would observe the obvious.

"He never leaves his car unlocked. Never," Helen whispered, as Burton sat behind the wheel. She watched him run his fingers quickly over the dashboard, and then lean across to the glove compartment. Flipping it open, he saw it was empty.

Stevens peered inside as well. "Keys?"

Burton shook his head. "No, I can't see them."

Shutting the compartment, Burton climbed out of the Audi and looked at the others. "It's clean. Somebody wiped it clean. His mobile is gone and looks like his satnav as well." Glancing through the windscreen, he looked back up at Helen. "It's been here four days and it's spotless."

"He was never *that* tidy." Stevens muttered.

"No, he wasn't. It's as if..."

"As if somebody comes and cleans it every day," Helen concluded for Stevens.

"Yes," Burton replied, slamming the Audi's door.

"What now?" Tara said.

Burton glanced towards the sign at the end of the car park. It indicated the way to the village of Helford. "We go into town."

"No!" Helen cried. She shook her head, looking up at the giant trees and the crows, cawing loudly. "Let's just get out of here."

"Helen," Stevens said firmly, "we can't leave him. Andrews would rubbish us so hard we'd all end up as bloody filing clerks. It's the crows bugging you, that's all. They'll stop soon."

"He's right," Burton said softly. "It's just the crows. We'll go straight to his B&B and fulfil the mission. We'll find out what he discovered. Then we get out. I promise. No more than a few hours."

"You promise?"

"Yes." He nodded.

Opening his jacket, Stevens pulled out a small, black, automatic 9 millimetre handgun. He rammed a clip into the pistol grip. Burton did the same with his.

"Do we you really need those?" Tara asked. Tall, thin with fair hair and a pale complexion, she peered over her glasses at Burton. "Do we really want to wave guns around?"

"A precaution only. You don't have to if you don't want to," Burton replied as he put his gun into the holster under his jacket.

Slowly, they moved across the car park, past a large sign indicating no cars were allowed in the village, down a curving, tree-lined, narrow road towards the river Hel.

Halfway down this picturesque road with Burton and Stevens a few paces ahead, Helen stopped, wrapped her arms around herself and shivered. "I'm not going any further."

"There's nothing to worry about, darling," Tara said softly, putting her arm around Helen's shoulders. "He's probably so enchanted by the place he forgot to call in."

Smiling, Burton walked back up to Helen. "It's probably all a wild goose chase; but we do need to be sure."

A few feet away, Stevens looked up at the tall trees above them, where the crows cawed and cawed without any let-up. Glancing round them he could see no sign of habitation, just a narrow track lined with trees and low vegetation.

It was the middle of the day, yet the sky was overcast and grey. A breeze, carrying cold air came up the steep, narrow road from the river below, which was not yet visible from their vantage point. At any other time or place, he thought, this would be a beautiful spot. Instead he couldn't help feeling a sense of foreboding. He looked back at the others.

"She's right. There's something about this place."

Firmly, Burton, took Helen's arm and walked her down the road, past Stevens. "The sooner we get down there the sooner we can get out. Alright."

Nodding, Stevens followed, with Tara beside him. "Okay," he said, "But don't expect me to relax." He checked his watch.

Slowly, they descended along the road to the edge of the river where they stopped and looked across to the village. Like most Cornish towns and villages, the buildings were old, whitewashed, two-storey structures crowded together and separated only by narrow streets. In some cases, the streets were so old the original cobblestones still existed.

They stood on a small stone causeway, the only way into the village. A tattered old sign tacked to a wooden pole beside the causeway indicated the river could only be crossed at low tide. Burton thought this was the reason no cars were allowed in the town. He checked his watch. "High tide in three hours. We need to be sure we're across in time or we're stuck here."

The causeway was just wide enough for pedestrians to pass across and a single vehicle at any one time. Once across, they entered the village moving down the main street towards the tiny harbour. There was only one street. The old, whitewashed houses almost all decorated with pretty flowers in window pots and flower troughs had all been built on the slope of the hill. Each seemed to have steep stairs leading to the front doors and scattered around there were paved lanes where cars could be carefully parked.

Although the village allowed no cars it was obvious

that the residents were allowed their own vehicles. Everyone else had to keep theirs out of the town. Convenient, thought Burton.

Across the causeway, Helen stopped again.

Puzzled, Burton stared at her, "What is it?" he asked.

"A feeling. Vague shapes nothing concrete." She looked up at Burton her eyes wide. "There's danger here, Joe."

Nodding, he squeezed her hand. "When the mission is complete, we'll leave."

Moving slowly down the street, they passed the post office with an old rusted metal Walls ice Cream sign outside. It swayed and creaked in the wind. It was the only sound they could hear, except for the crows on the other side of the river.

Beside the post office a grey house, with a large picture window called Tresilick Cottage, advertised for bed and breakfast. A handwritten sign in the window indicated home-made Cornish Cream fudge for sale.

As they walked, Helen felt sure the curtains in each house they passed moved slightly as if their progress was being monitored. This place looks lovely, she thought, but it feels evil.

In the centre of the village, above the harbour, they saw all the buildings were so old they had thatched roofs.

25

Burton stopped outside the oldest building in the village, the Shipwright Inn. It's old, thick, plastered walls, gleamed with fresh white paint.

"This is the place," Burton said, surveying the area. "His text said he had a room at the Shipwright."

They looked at each other, then Tara giggled slightly. "Who knows, maybe he's at the bar completely rat-arsed."

"He never drinks," Helen said sharply. "Not like that."

Shrugging, Tara smiled. "It was only a joke."

"Forget it," Burton cut in. "Let's get this over with. Come on."

Taking Helen by the hand Burton led her through the old, low, oak door into the pub followed by Tara and Stevens. The conversations the few customers were making stopped abruptly and all eyes swivelled to the newcomers.

Again, like the rest of the town, the pub was quaint and lovely, with old world charm oozing from the dark mahogany beams lining the ceiling, the framed prints and paintings of ships covering every available inch of wall space. There were two large ship bells at each end of the bar, which ran alongside the entire left wall between the entrance and the exit to the patio overlooking the beautiful, natural harbour. It was dark, dimly lit by low electric lamps in simulated 19th Century ship lanterns hanging on the old wooden pillars throughout the pub. At the far end a set of creaking, old wooden stairs led the way up to the rooms above.

As they walked towards the bar, the conversation from the four locals sitting at a table by the fire and two heavyset men at the end of the bar, who slowly turned their eyes away, began to ebb and flow again. Helen knew they might appear to be taking no notice; but these people were keeping one eye and one ear on every word she and her companions said. She could feel it, in every part of her, she could feel the menace, burning through her skin as they watched her. She turned away, droplets of sweat rolling down her back. Yet she wasn't hot.

"We've got to get out of here," she whispered, a lump in her throat as hysteria began to rise. "We must go," she croaked, insistent. "We are in danger. I can feel it."

Burton, stroked her hand gently as they waited at the bar. "Relax," he said through smiling teeth as the barmaid approached. "We won't be long."

"What can I get 'ee, today?"

"Two bitters and two shandies." Burton said, smiling, pulling out his money.

"God, that looks delightful," Stevens said, wiping his mouth and watching the barmaid pour the beer.

Quietly, Burton whispered to Stevens, "We are not

drinking this. It's just to make a good impression."

"Speak for yourself," Stevens' big hand grabbed his full glass and brought it quickly to his eager lips. In one gulp half its contents had gone down his throat. He let out a satisfied sigh. "That just makes my day."

Smiling, Burton turned to the barmaid. "We're looking for someone, a friend of ours."

"Ye be London folk same as your friend?"

"Er.. yes. He's supposed to be staying here."

"Mr Harrington?"

Nodding, Burton grinned. "Yes, that's right. Do you know where he is?"

Indicating the stairs at the far end of the room, the girl looked at Burton briefly, looked over his shoulder and glanced away. "His room is number 13, up the stairs."

Quickly, she scurried away to serve two of the locals sitting at the bar. Helen trembled, seeing the suspicion in the faces of the two old and wizened men. Both men spoke in low tones together glancing several times in her direction.

Was her mind playing tricks, she wondered? Ever since they lost contact with Harrington she had not slept. Running this investigation had been wrong from the beginning. She'd felt it. Never before had she been *so* strongly opposed to anything as she had to this. Glancing at her companions she wondered how they could be so blind to the terror lying under the surface of this sleepy village.

Stevens drained his glass with a satisfied grin and motioned to the stairs. "I believe she said up there?"

"Room 13," Burton replied. "Let's go."

The Barmaid returned. "Would 'ee like me to take you up?"

"That would be very kind; if it's no bother."

"Tidn't no bother at all. I'm happy to do it. Just 'ee wait while I make sure I've got cover here." She slipped away into the room behind the bar taking off her apron as she did so. Burton could hear voices muffled coming from the door she'd left ajar when she suddenly returned through the door followed by two large bearded men. The tallest of the two had a thatch of grey hair that looked as if it had never seen a comb. While he had a pleasant face it was offset by the coldest eyes Burton had ever seen. Also, under his floppy sweater both Burton and Stevens could see that the man was athletically built.

The second, smaller man, was similar to the other only he was younger and where he lacked height his physique was that of a boxer. As the Barmaid came out from behind the bar she motioned to the two men. "My uncle Jim 'ere owns the pub, and he'll take over while I see you all upstairs and settled." Motioning to the younger man, "Cousin Alfie will help out as well, won't you dear?"

The man grunted an inaudible reply. "Now if you folks just follow me, I'll show you Mr Harrington's room."

She bustled quickly up the stairs beside the bar when Alfie stood in front of Burton and stared at him. "Eee best not stay long."

"Oh, and why is that?"

"On account of the ghost, see?"

"Ghost?" Burton stared back at Alfie.

"'Ehs. Everyone's afraid cept'n me an Jim, 'ere," Alfie spat. "Eee won't last long."

"Thanks for the advice." Burton quickly brushed past Alfie followed by the others. On the floor above the stairs led into an L-shaped hallway for the inn's 14 rooms. 13 was at the far end of the building, the foot of the L. The barmaid knocked on the door several times; but as there was no answer she looked at Burton and the others. "I reckon 'ee be out now, but you're all welcome to wait for him and get yourselves settled in. I've got rooms 6 & 5 available for you."

"That's very kind," Burton smiled. "But could you let us into Mr Harrington's room?"

"Well, I oughtn't, it being his room an' all."

"It would really help us out and we would be very grateful."

The Barmaid hesitated for a few moments looking at Burton, Stevens, Tara and finally, Helen. Burton added, motioning to Helen, "I should have mentioned, this is Mr Harrington's fiancé".

"Oh, you should've said! I know how it is, you haven't heard from him and you've come down because you're worried. Don't blame 'ee, as Mr Harrington's a fine looking man."

As she talked the barmaid had taken out a cluster of keys, fumbled through them and then inserted one into the lock and opened the door to room 13. She stood aside, letting the others enter first, then followed them in. Standing at the door, she looked at Burton and then Helen. "If you want anything just call down to the bar, and Jim or me will help."

Stevens touched the barmaid's arm. "What was all that about a ghost?"

Turning to Stevens, who towered over her, she flushed as she looked up at him. "Oh, pay Alfie no mind. It's just talk is all."

Stevens nodded as Burton stepped forward. "What's your name, then?"

"Jade."

"A lovely name. Thank you, Jade. If we need anything we'll let you know." Handing her some money she looked at it with a puzzled expression, quickly smiled and then left closing the door behind her.

The room was rectangular with a bed, night table,

dresser and wardrobe, adjacent to a small sitting area, with two chairs, and a table by a large picture window at the other end. Opposite the sitting area was the door to the bathroom. The usual mediocre paintings of meadows, sunsets and forests dotted the walls.

Burton stood in the centre of the room and looked around, as Stevens moved to the window while the two women sat on the bed. "Right everyone, search it inside out."

The room was spotless. Harrington's luggage lay on the desk where he'd left it. Burton quickly searched through that while the others searched the rest of the room. Except Stevens, who remained at the window.

Within ten minutes of Burton's command, Tara spoke. "Got something."

While searching the wardrobe she'd run her fingers up along the inside of the lip of the door and in the corner her fingers came upon a tiny package that had been put there with cellotape. "I was thinking this room was too clean and that if Harrington had hidden anything here, it'd been found."

"So why didn't they check the wardrobe?" Burton said.

"They probably did but it looks like Harrington has really jammed whatever this is in the corner. If you didn't know his ways you'd miss it for sure." From her jacket

32

pocket Tara pulled out a penknife, reached up and cut the tiny package away from the wardrobe. Moving to the desk, the others gathered round her, except for Stevens, as she cut away the cellotape and packaging revealing a small SDHC card used primarily for storing images taken with digital cameras.

Picking up the card, Burton looked it over for a moment, then handed it to Tara. "Your laptop read this type of card?"

"It does."

Quickly, Tara pulled a small laptop from her bag, placed it on the table, turned it on and then put the card into the card reader on the side of the machine. A few minutes later they were staring at the files and images on the card. "Our Harrington has been busy," Tara said.

Standing behind her, Burton watched her scroll slowly through the hundreds of images and files. He pointed to a folder. "Open that folder." Tara double clicked on the folder and suddenly the screen was filled with a list of documents all encoded except for one, which she opened. "Looks like Harrington has been keeping track of activity here. It's a spread sheet, dates, times, places, pick-ups and deliveries. Merchandise of some sort."

"Yeah, but what merchandise? Could be anything."

Tara looked up at Burton. "Well, we can be pretty sure it's illegal. The rest of it is encrypted. It'll take a few minutes for the computer to decode it."

'Move away from the computer!'

Startled, Burton and Tara turned quickly, suddenly realising that Helen was not with them. Instead, she now stood a few paces away with a gun levelled at Burton's chest.

"I said step away from the computer."

"Helen, what the hell is this?" Burton said quietly. "Put the gun down."

"I want the SD card and the computer."

For a moment Burton stared at her, weighing up the situation. The hand that held the gun was rock steady but in her eyes he saw a glimpse of uncertainty.

"Helen, don't make me take the gun from you."

"You'd be dead before you reached me, now give me the computer."

Glancing at Tara, Burton nodded. "Give it to her."

Turning off the laptop, Tara suddenly stood up. "What about all that crap about you saying there was danger here, evil here and that we should leave? Was that all shit?

"Oh no, she does have the gift, don't you, Helen?"

"Yes, I do," Helen said, switching her glance to Tara. "And I am sick of working for a selfish, incompetent, uncaring government while being poor the whole time."

For a moment the room was filled with silence and

everyone remained still. Suddenly, Tara closed the lid of the laptop and picked it up from the desk, turning to Helen. "What's on this card that's so important?"

"Never mind, just give me the computer, with the card still in the reader, if you please."

Tara stepped forward with the laptop in her hand. From the corner of his eye, Burton caught sight of Stevens moving quickly away from the window towards Helen. She had seen it too and, suddenly, swivelled to cover him with her gun. At that moment, Burton quickly stepped forward, grabbed Helen's gun arm and pushed it up her back, then hit her on the back of the neck with two quick chops. Like a house of cards, she crumbled to the floor, unconscious.

Taking the gun from her hand, he looked up at Tara. "Put her on the bed and tie her up then get back on that computer and find out what that was all about."

Tara nodded as Burton stood up, pocketing Helen's gun and glancing at Stevens. "Took your time, don't you think?"

"I was waiting for the right moment."

Grabbing Helen under the arms, Tara hauled her onto the bed, rolling her onto her stomach. From her bag, Tara pulled out some plastic cord normally used for tying up electrical cable. Within moments she had Helen's arms behind her back and her hands and feet bound. She then moved back to the desk with the laptop and turned it on.

Running his hands through his hair, Burton straightened his jacket and joined Stevens at the window. "Nice view?"

Stevens handed Burton a tiny pair of field glasses. "Look five degrees west from the harbour entrance and you'll see a tiny island."

The window had a commanding view of the village harbour, the harbour entrance and the sea beyond, as well as the quay and little shops that lined the road around the harbour. A fine low mist had rolled in since they'd arrived.

"I see it. About a mile out, I would guess."

"Do you see the structure on it?"

Burton peered through the glasses, smaller than opera glasses but far more powerful. He could see the island was more a rock outcropping with cliffs that stood about 100 feet above the sea. On top of the cliffs was the only vegetation that he could see and behind the low trees he could see an old stone tower. "I see a structure of some sort. Maybe an old castle."

"That island is only big enough for that one tower."

"So?"

"The harbour is empty of people, the shops are shut, there seems to be no movement at all, except for one place, the dock."

Burton trained the glasses on the harbour quay a few yards from the inn. Ropes, tackle, chains crates could be seen where throughout the rest of the harbour none of that, or any other activity, was in evidence. A black van sat at the road end of the dock. Burton looked back at Stevens. "Get to the point."

"All the boats in the harbour are small fishing vessels except for one, which is much larger than anything else. It comes into the dock and ties up there. No other vessel is anywhere near the dock. This particular boat seems to be sailing between here and the island. It's done the trip twice since I've been watching. Takes about ten minutes each way and it stays over on the island for about 20 minutes, then it comes back and does the whole thing over again. It's on its way back now."

Looking out at the harbour and the island beyond it, Burton tried searching through the mist to see any sign of a ship heading towards the harbour but he saw nothing. "It does sound strange."

"Whatever's going on here, boss, I think is on that island and that is where we need to be. If we're going to find Harrington, then I think that's where he is."
Burton looked up at Stevens. "Harrington did what he was trained to do and left us the information. He knew the risks."

"Of course, but I think it would be worth our while to check that island out anyway."
Burton shook his head. "No. We get the card decoded,

check the information on it, do what we have to and leave. Finding Harrington is not top priority."

"I've got something," Tara said, looking at the files on the laptop.

"What," said Burton moving to her. He and Stevens gathered behind her as they all looked at the laptop and the files that Tara was slowly going through. "Lot's of images mostly taken at night, documents and some video too. Hard to see what is what though but," she pointed to a couple of images on the screen, "it looks like that is the boat that Stevens was talking about."

Burton nodded. "Have you checked any of the documents?"

She shook her head. "No, just looked at the images."

For a moment, Burton was silent, thoughtful, then he patted Tara's shoulder. "Keep at it. I particularly want to know why Helen turned on us." Turning to Stevens he said, "You and I need to start asking awkward questions". Turing back to Tara he added, "Keep your mobile on the encrypted channel".

Suddenly, there was knock at the door.

Moving quickly, Burton pulled out his gun and held it by his side and opened the door. Without warning, Jade suddenly barged into the room followed by Aflie and Jim, both with shotguns. Alfie pointed his shotgun at Burton's chest. "Put the gun on the floor and kick it over here."

Burton did as he was told.

Jade glanced at Burton then over to Tara who had twisted around in her chair. Motioning with her pistol she said, "Turn off the laptop, stand up, put it on the table then go stand at the window with your back to it". She turned to Burton. "You join her."

As Tara closed the laptop and placed it on the bed, Burton moved to the window. "I notice your accent is gone. You should be in the theatre," he said amiably. "Everything else fake as well? Your name for example?"

"Jade is my name." She looked at Tara. "Get over to the window."

Burton nodded. "Got the place wired I suppose?"

"Yes. I'm surprised you people didn't discover the cameras."

"Yes," Burton replied, drily. "So am I."

On the bed, Helen stirred.

Suddenly, Jade's eyes widened. "Where's the tall one?"

"Here!" Stevens flung the bathroom door open, dropped to a crouch, gun in hand, and fired three shots. Alfie and Jim were dead before they hit the floor, each with a bullet in the forehead. The third shot hit Jade in the shoulder, spinning her around forcing her to drop the gun. She screamed and fell to the floor, clutching her shoulder.

Blood oozed from the wound. She looked up at Stevens. "The other one didn't carry a gun."

"We do," Burton said as he knelt down beside her, looking at her wound. Breathing hard, Jade's face was white and she gritted her teeth from the pain, tears flowing down her face. Tara bent down beside Burton looking at Jade's wound. "I can stop the bleeding and bind it up." She looked up at Stevens. "Get me my bag on that table."

Stevens nodded, collected her bag from the table and handed it to her. From it she pulled a small first aid kit and began to work on Jade's wound as Burton spoke.

"I want some answers. What are you in to here?"

Gasping, her face contorted with pain, Jade looked up at Burton. "Drugs mostly and people, girls for overseas buyers. We gave them a life overseas, riches, comfort."

"While getting them hooked on drugs."

"No, drugs come in. Girls go out."

"Where are they?"

Her face contorted with pain, Jade struggled to get the words out. "All on the island." Suddenly, her eyes rolled up into her head as she slipped into unconsciousness.

Standing Burton looked down at Tara. "Give her something for the pain. I need her awake."

Several hours later, as the mist and drizzle rolled slowly into the harbour, Burton stood on the dock looking up at

Stevens, gun in hand, who had just shot the two crew members of the largest boat in the harbour. Stevens stood outside the wheelhouse door, which hung open. The boat was a small coastal vessel originally built for carrying passengers about the size of a large executive yacht and had two decks. Most of the seats of the lower deck had been taken out so that cargo could be easily loaded. The upper deck, much shorter than the lower, still had its seats. The business part of the ship, from which both decks extended, was where the wheelhouse, radio, radar rooms, galley, tiny crew quarters and stores were all housed. The wheelhouse was higher than the upper deck, its roof bristling with antennae and instruments for modern navigation. On either side of the wheelhouse was a gangway leading down to both decks. The ship, if it could be called that, could be easily handled by three or four people.

However, in this case, there were only two and they both sat huddled in the corner of the wheelhouse with bullet holes in them. Stevens had shot one in the arm and the other in the hand as they had been uncooperative and the latter had been reaching for a gun.

On the dock, Burton surveyed the dead town and then quickly climbed aboard. On the lower deck, Tara, Helen, and Jade, stood huddled together. They all moved to the upper deck and found seats. Burton remained standing. He looked at the two women sitting in front of him. Helen, still groggy, now had only her hands bound, Tara had cut the cords around her feet when she'd regained consciousness. Jade, her wound now bandaged and her arm in a sling, was also a little sluggish from the painkillers Tara had given her.

The engine had not been switched off and still rumbled throughout the vessel. Burton saw Stevens run down the gangway and cast off as they got under way.

As they slowly moved away from the dock, Stevens entered through the door at the end of the upper deck and joined the others. "We're all ship shape," he said.

"What about those two upstairs?"

Stevens smiled holding up his gun. "I told them I would shoot them in other parts of their bodies if they didn't do exactly what they were told."

"They need medical attention?" Tara picked up her bag, ready to head outside.

Stevens nodded. "They will do, but let's get to the island first, then you can bandage them up all you like. I'll just go and check on them." With that he was gone back through the door and up the gangway to the wheelhouse as Tara sat beside Jade.

"Don't go to the island. Take us back," Jade whispered.

Burton's eyes narrowed. "Why?"

"No one goes there. Turn back," she whispered. Burton shook his head. "No. You need to start giving me some straight answers."

Her face was pale and drawn. Burton wasn't sure if it was from the pain of her wound or from fear but he looked at her as she moved gingerly and glanced up at him.

"Only Jim and Alfie ever went to the island. They took lots of guns. At the end of the quay there's a little house, or hut, and behind that are stairs that lead up to the top of the cliffs. Jim and Alfie only ever went to the hut."

"What else?"

"They put all the girls in the hut before they were shipped out and the drugs that came in were put in the hut as well. Your friend documented this before we realised who he was."

"Harrington?"

She nodded. "He hid the information and we couldn't find it. You have enough there to put us all away forever."

"How big is the organisation?'

"There are a few other villages along the coast and one or two people in London who helped us get the girls and gave us information on what the police and drug enforcement CID were doing."

"How did you find the girls?"

Jade shifted uncomfortably in her seat then spoke slowly with effort. "We put ads in the papers for modelling jobs in Cornwall and they came to us."

By this time the boat had left the harbour and was now ploughing through the open sea towards the island. As it rode the waves, Burton considered the information Jade had just told him, then he motioned to Helen. "What about her? How does she fit into this?"

"She put the ads in the papers, gave us information on the girls that applied, but most importantly, told us what the authorities were doing so we knew when to bring the drugs in and ship the girls out."

Burton stared at Jade then glared at Helen. "This true?"

Helen nodded. "I gave them times, dates, and places where the drug enforcement people would be so they could avoid them."

Looking at Helen, Burton realised the enormity of what she'd done. They all had access to sensitive information from sister government agencies and it was to be kept classified and secret. Every agent was thoroughly vetted, signed the Official Secrets Act, and became part of the close knit community of secret government agencies. Helen had betrayed that.

"This what Harrington had on you?"

"He hacked into my laptop at work and left for here

before I could get to him."

At that moment, Stevens put his head in the door and said. "Five minutes."

Nodding, Burton turned to Tara. "Get these two ready for disembarking."

"No," Jade grabbed Burton's arm. "Turn back. You've got everything you need."

Ignoring her he turned back to Tara. "Get them ready," then he quickly left and joined Stevens outside on the lower deck.

Moments later they stood on the long stone quay that had been built out from the island shore at the base of the cliff, the boat moored alongside. As Jade had said, there was a hut made of stone, at the island end of the quay, and built into the cliff-face were steps of stone and concrete that led up to the cliff tops. The steps were shrouded in a wire mesh fence with a heavy locked gate at the bottom beside the hut.

The two crew members and two women stood unhappily in front of the hut with Stevens and Tara facing them, their guns trained on the four prisoners. In front of the wooden door of the hut, Burton looked at the lock, then turned to Jade. "Open it."

She shook her head. "I don't have the keys."

From her bag, slung over her shoulder, Tara pulled

out a small purse. "They're here. I took them off her when she was shot." She threw the purse over to Burton who caught it, extracted a set of keys, and handed them to Jade. "Open it."

Reluctantly and painfully, Jade unlocked the door and was suddenly propelled roughly through it by Burton, who pushed Helen and the two crew members into the darkened hut after her. From his inside pocket, Burton pulled out a torch and flicked it on just as Stevens and Tara did with theirs.

Inside the hut were several cots jammed together in one corner. Most of these cots were empty except for two. The occupants were young girls, dishevelled and from their lack of movement, apparently drugged. Burton motioned to the two crew members. "Get them onto them onto the ship." To Tara he said, "Make sure they do it gently and make the girls comfortable. If these two try anything shoot them."

Tara nodded and got the crew members busy, transferring the drugged girls from the hut to the boat, her gun trained on them at all times.

Stevens and Burton now looked at the rest of the items in the hut. Wooden crates lined one wall stacked from floor to ceiling. Stevens raised his eyebrows, "Drugs?"

Jade nodded. "Some weapons too."

"Jesus." Burton waved his gun towards the door motioning for everyone to leave the hut. Outside Stevens spoke to him. "What do we do with the drugs?"

"Load it on the ship." Turning to Jade, Burton pointed his gun directly at her head. "Where is Harrington?"

"Up top," said Jade, motioning to the steps.

"Is that where the rest of the towns people are?"

"Yes," she breathed, wincing with the effort. "I need to sit down. I need medical attention."

"You lied about Jim and Alfie not going up to the top, didn't you?"Jade said nothing. "What else have you lied about?"

"Nothing, I swear."

Burton and Stevens now stood facing Helen and Jade. "Let's find out then. Open the gate."

Jade turned to the gate and then back to Burton. "No. I mean, I can't."

"Open it. You've got the keys, so open it."

Over the sound of the sea lapping against the shore and the waves crashing against the quay a shot was heard from the boat. Startled, Burton turned suddenly towards the boat, when Tara appeared at the lower deck, gun in hand.

"All OK?"

Smiling, Tara replied, "One of them jumped over the

side".

"Did you hit him," Stevens asked.

"I think so."

Turning back to Jade, Burton propelled her through the now open wire mesh gate, then took Helen roughly be the arm and pushed her through as well. "Climb," he said.

Slowly the two women climbed the steps, clinging onto the wire mesh as they did.

A few minutes later they reached the top of the steps where there was another wire gate, also locked. Burton jammed his gun into Jade's back. "Open it and give me the keys."

She did as she was told and was then pushed through the open gate by Burton with Helen being pushed by Stevens. Burton locked the gate behind him. Fear filled Jade's face as she turned to Burton. "Why did you do that? You'll get us all killed."

Ignoring her, Burton looked around him. Stevens had been right. The island was very small. It was essentially an outcrop of rock that over the centuries had acquired vegetation in the form of stunted windswept trees, wild grass and shrubs. Virtually in the centre of the island was a large stone structure that was a house at the base with a two storey tower rising up from the middle of it.

The wind pushed the thickening mist and drizzle across the top of the island, bending the trees against its force. Suddenly on the wind came a terrible, wail, unearthly and low. Jade shivered and clutched Helen's arm. Burton and Stevens stared at each other, then Burton said to the women, "Let's go".

They moved towards the structure, following a path through the trees and undergrowth.

Suddenly, Jade stumbled and nearly fell. Helen held her up. Looking down at what she'd stumbled over, Jade recoiled with horror. On the path were the remains of a man who had been half eaten.

Covering his mouth and nose with his arm, Burton leaned over the mangled body.

"Christ what a stink," said Stevens, recoiling. After a moment he stepped forward, "Any ID?"

"From his clothes I'd say it was Harrington. His face is so badly mangled, it's hard to say."

"Christ," Stevens swore. "Harrington, you poor guy."

"Mourn for him later," Burton said. "We've got to keep going."

"We can't leave him," Helen whispered.

"I'm sorry about your friend," Jade said.

Another wail pierced the wind, followed by another. This time, they were much closer.

"We keep going," said Burton, standing.

"No, we have to get out of here. You've found what you wanted. We must go," Jade said breathlessly. "We've got to go!"

"No, we go forward." Burton motioned for Jade to move up the path. Again, the women moved along the path towards the structure with Burton and Stevens following, their guns levelled at each of the women.

As they moved forward, Stevens thought he saw movement from the corner of his eye. Dark shapes moving near to them. He checked his gun nervously.
Suddenly, another wail sounded, this time very near, again followed by another and another.

Reaching the building, Burton saw that the windows had been smashed and the door hung off its hinges. The smell of rotting flesh and faeces filled his nostrils, making him gag. The two women were already being sick nearby. Underfoot the ground had become slimy and soft.

"Christ, I'm not going in there," Stevens wretched.

Before Burton could reply, the wails started up again; but this time with added ferocity and low growls. From the mist, dark shapes suddenly emerged moving quickly towards them, loping across the ground.

Stevens dropped to his knees and fired at the shapes.

From the building, something rushed out and Helen screamed as its huge jaws and teeth bit into her shoulder. Her blood splattered all over Jade, who now screamed uncontrollably.

Burton twisted quickly, firing several shots; but Helen was gone. Her screams could be heard as she was dragged away. Over Jade's screams, Burton could hear Stevens firing. "Back to the gate!" He yelled.

Grabbing Jade's arm, Burton pulled her down the path, running back towards the gate with Stevens behind him. On either side he was aware of the creatures matching their speed. Suddenly, one jumped down from a tree in front of them, its huge jaws snapping hungrily. Burton could see the razor sharp teeth glistening in the mist, its glowing eyes staring at him. Without breaking his stride he shot the creature and it fell away from the path.

Suddenly Burton stumbled over a rock in the path, losing his grip on Jade's arm. She fell into the shrubs beside the path and instantly two creatures jumped on her, their jaws and teeth tearing and ripping into her. As she screamed, Burton and Stevens fired at the creatures; but they were too fast and had dragged Jade away into the scrub and mist seemingly unaffected by the bullets.

"I thought I hit them both," Stevens said catching his breath. "I couldn't have missed."

"Forget it. We've got to go." Burton pulled the empty clip from his pistol and rammed in a full one he'd taken from his jacket. Stevens did the same. As they did so, the wailing began again all around them, mingled with growling and spitting.

They could see shapes moving in the mist coming towards them. Burton fired a shot at a shape directly in front of him as he ran down the path. Behind he heard Stevens fire two shots. They ran. Jumping over rocks, sliding in the mud and slime as they headed for the gate.

Moments later they reached it, panting for breath. Burton fumbled with Jade's keys, trying to find the right one. They could hear the growling and snarling of the creatures coming closer. One jumped out of the mist towards them and was quickly shot down by Stevens. It disappeared into the mist.

"Hurry up!" Stevens fired another shot at two creatures coming at him. They quickly melted away. "They're getting closer."

"I know."

"Really close!"

"I know!"

Burton tried the fifth key in the lock and suddenly it turned. "Got it!" Yanking the gate open they moved quickly through and then slammed the thing shut.

"Lock it!"

As Burton put the key in the lock, the creatures swarmed all over the gate and his hands were torn from teeth and razor sharp claws. He felt the weight of the creatures against the gate and, just behind him, the sound of Stevens firing filled his ears. Finally, the lock clicked and he turned and pounded down the stairs followed by Stevens.

Half way down they heard the gate above suddenly smash open, which gave them both the urge to go down the winding twisting steps much faster. At the bottom gate, Burton handed his gun to Stevens as he fumbled to find the key to open it. Stevens raced up a few steps until he saw the creatures coming down.

Kneeling he fired both guns at them. Shot after shot, each one hitting a creature. They came at him through the mist, along the wire mesh walls and roof, down the steps, their bodies piling up with each shot. As each magazine emptied Stevens pulled out another from his jacket ramming them into the pistols as they emptied with well-timed precision.

Suddenly, from below, Stevens heard Burton. "It's open!"

He raced down the few steps and flew through the gate that Burton slammed shut behind him. He heard the heavy click of the lock. Turning he threw Burton his gun and both men stood in front of the gate, firing through the mesh at the creatures, now just shapes in the mist. After a few minutes they stopped firing. There was no sign of movement just thickening heavy mist and drizzle.

The creatures were gone.

Both men stood by the gate gasping for breath

soaked from head to toe. They looked at each other. "What the hell was that all about?"

"I don't know," Burton said. "But we better call it in." From his jacket he pulled out his mobile phone and checked it. "No signal though."

"There's a ship to shore phone on the boat."

Nodding, Burton clicked on the safety catch of his pistol and put it back in its holster. He caught sight of something jammed between the side of the wire mesh that covered the steps and the rocks. Bending down he grabbed it and tugged. Stevens helped. After several attempts they finally pulled out a rusted, twisted metal sign that had probably once been on the gate. It read: WARNING! HAZARDOUS MATERIAL! DANGER, KEEP OUT! BY ORDER OF THE MINISTRY OF DEFENCE.

"Well, I guess that explains a lot," Stevens said. "Another failed project? Christ if this ever gets out…. If *they* ever get out!"

The two men just stared at each in silence.

After a moment, Burton picked up the sign and hurled it into the sea, watching it float for a few moments before it sank below the surface. He looked up at Stevens. "Let's get the hell out of here. Call it in, Frank. We need to get the clean-up boys down here, and fast."

"One thing though." Stevens looked at the locked fence then back to Burton. "What happened to the people?

Could they be…? I mean, was there something else….?"

Burton shook his head, unwilling to think about the answer. "Let's get the hell out of here."

The two men walked quickly down the quay towards the ship. As he was about to climb aboard, Burton stopped and looked back at the gate. A shiver went down his spine. Over the sound of the sea he could have sworn he heard a low wail coming from end of the quay near the hut. Or was it just the wind?

Initiation Day

Rain. A slight drizzle, spitting only, began to fall gently from the overcast sky.

"Happy birthday, Pete."

Sheri, the girl of his dreams, whispered softly as she sat on the crumbling wall of the grave-yard surrounding the old church of St Peter's in the Forest. Her words filled his thoughts with joy. She cares, he thought. There is hope. Sheri, the blonde beauty that tormented his dreams and thoughts was 16, beautiful, deliciously built and spoken for.

That was Peter Harper's cross.

But is she happy? he wondered.

Ordinarily, girls that went with Mick Traynor the leader of the local gang would never give him a second glance; but she had spoken to him, and few days before smiled at him, in school. Mick was 18, rode a motor-cycle and was Sheri's lover; of that he was sure. Mick was bigger than Harper, stronger and good-looking. His leather jacket, jeans, wavy short cropped hair, cigarette in the corner of his mouth, gave him the air of a pop star. That he sang in a local rock band also didn't help.

Peter had none of those. Just an ordinary git, he thought. No wonder no girl bothered to look at him. He was just 16 and rode a bicycle.

"Let's do something," Sheri said softly to Mick, sharing his cigarette.

"Like what?" Mick replied, taking the cigarette from her.

She shrugged. "Go to Joe's?"

The Church, situated on the edge of Epping Forest, had woods all around it. As darkness closed in from approaching night, they swayed in the slowly building wind, the sweet song-birds of the day giving way to the eerie sounds of night.

"I got no money," Scobie, another gang member said.

"I'm not paying for you, again." Alf, Mick's closest friend, responded.

Peter watched Sheri look up at the night, shiver, and put her arm around Mick's. Glancing quickly at his watch he knew he should be indoors. His parents would soon realise he wasn't home and would begin to worry.

"I'm cold." Sheri whispered.

God, he wished he was Mick. Something in his expression must have caught the older boy's eye because Mick stared directly at him. "It's Petey's birthday today. He's not a little boy anymore." Jumping off the wall he moved towards Peter. "What does the little boy want for his birthday?"

Peter shrugged. "Nothing, forget it."

Suddenly Mick grabbed Pete's shirt, pulling him off the wall onto the grass, snarling. "Don't tell me what to do."

Staring at each other for a moment, Mick suddenly straightened. "I need a slash." Turning, he headed off towards the Church followed by Scobie, Alf and the rest of the gang, to the Church wall where Mick was already relieving himself.

Peter moved to Sheri. "If I didn't have a bike and I was a member of the gang, would you like me better?"

"I dunno," she said. "Yeah, Maybe."

"What's this?" Mick's voice floated towards them as he returned, putting his hands on Sheri's knees. "Is this little boy bothering you?"

"He wants to be a member of the gang."

"Does he?" Mick said, smiling at Peter, slowly circling him. "Well, there is an initiation that all gang members have to go through."

"What?" Alf looked up, from the stuck zip of his jeans.

Annoyed, Mick motioned for him to stay quiet and continued as Peter kept his eyes on Sheri.

"Everyone here has done it. Lot's of little boys have tried; but little boys just don't make it. When night comes all kinds of weird things can happen in the forest." He stared at Peter then shook his head. "And little boys just wimp out."

Peter tore his eyes away from Sheri. He had been looking at her legs that Mick had touched, longing to stroke them. Her skirts were always very short and he longed to touch her creamy smooth skin. He shuddered slightly and looked at Mick. "What things?"

"I've heard strange noises in the woods at night. Grunts, growls, hissing, spitting, odd noises. There's something out here and I saw it on my initiation day and I survived."

"Yeah?" Peter said, more and more interested.

Sitting on a gravestone of cracked, caked marble, Mick continued looking around at the group. "I stood on top of this dead old tree trunk and I heard voices. I saw shadows moving in the woods and inside the Church."

Suppressed laughter suddenly turned to coughing from Alf as the others, also hiding grins and smirks, also turned away. None of this seemed to get through to Peter. This was his chance to join the gang and be close to Sheri who never left his thoughts.

"What did you do?" he whispered.

"I said the oath and left."

Peter nodded. "So you just climbed on top of a tree?"

Nodding, suppressing laughter by clearing his throat, Mick glanced directly at Peter. "The thing is you have to be naked."

"Naked?"

More choking and laughter form the others.

"Yeah, and when you get to the top you stand there and shout the gang oath."

"What oath?"

Holding back his laughter, Mick looked away at the others, motioning them to keep quiet. He looked back at Peter. "Warriors Rule!"

"That's It?"

Smiling Mick nodded. "Yeah, that's it."

Looking from Mick to Sheri who was examining her shoes. He thought, it could be a joke; but if it gets me closer to her then fine.

"Where is this tree?"

Mick stood up. "Ah, deep in the woods, near the pond. There's a big bush of nettles all around it. You have to find a way through the nettles to get to the old tree. When you do, you climb up the tree and stand on top of the trunk. Then you say the oath."

Peter took a deep breath as the others stood up, moving closer to him.

"You gonna do it, Pete," asked Alf, coughing to hide his laughter?

He looked at Sheri who looked back at him, crossing her legs. "Why don't you, Pete. You've got nothing to lose."

Mick turned away, looking at the others. "It's obvious he wants to stay a little boy. He says he wants to be one of us but look at him..."

Pete sucked in some air and cleared his throat. "When?"

Picking up can of beer Mick pulled off the top and drank heavily. "Tomorrow night. Midnight." He finally said belching and wiping his mouth with his sleeve. "We meet here first. No torches. Torches are for little boys, so are bicycles."

"I'll be here." Peter said, moving towards the forest out of the church Grounds.

Suddenly, Mick called after him. "Petey!"

Peter stopped, looking back at him. "You want to prove you're a big boy, don't you?"

He heard their laughter as he picked up his bicycle and headed along the narrow path through the forest towards home. Their laughter echoed in his ears. Mick was right, the forest at night seemed strange and frightening. Hurrying along he hoped he would overcome his fear and go through with it. A tear rolled slowly down his cheek as he remembered their laughter. He would do it. To be a wimp, to always be known as being afraid, would be impossible to live with.

"You're daft if you do this, Peetsy." Jason watched Peter play Attack Run, a simulated air attack, game on his laptop as rock music blasted from the stereo in the corner of his room later that evening.

"It's just one night then I'm closer to Her forever!"

"She's not worth it."

"Shit!" Peter smashed his hand on the joystick after being shot down half way through bombing run. Moving out of the seat he sat on the bed. "You try."

Taking over, Jason began a new game talking as he played. "I mean you can see her in school everyday. Why get involved with a bunch of losers like Mick and Alf?"

"Because I can't get her out of my mind."

Glancing at his friend, Jason smiled. "You've got the hots for her. Once you've screwed her she won't be that important. Trust me."

"You're an expert are you?"

"I know."

"Piss off." Peter snorted as Jason, too, was shot down in mid-run.

Shrugging Jason moved out of his seat, "I was distracted by you. I can beat it any day."

The music reached a climax as Peter moved into the chair vacated by Jason. "It doesn't matter, I'm going to do it. Even if I get her for just one night it'll be worth it."

"Has she promised you, has she said if you do this I will sleep with you?"

"Not exactly, but..."

"There you go...." Jason trailed off picking up one of Peter's models and looking at the exquisite detail. "I got the new Airfix Spitfire yesterday. Want to come over and take a look at it?"

"Models are for kids."

"They are not. There's loads of old gits who do them in their 30's. My dad does one on occasion. I think you're seriously deranged by this girl."

"Shut up! I'm going to do it and that's all."

Jason nodded, sitting on the bed watching Peter go through his bombing run. "Told your Dad yet?"

"No."

"What are you going to do? Sneak out?"

"I dunno. I dunno. I'll think of something."

Realising Peter no longer wanted to talk, Jason stood up, "I have to go. See you". Grabbing his jacket from the back of a chair already covered in clothes he quickly left just as Peter's bombing run failed yet again.

Sitting back he stared at the two words flashing on the screen. Game Over. Game Over. After a moment, he lay on the bed thinking of Sheri's smooth, creamy thighs that so often showed when she crossed her legs in her short skirts. He thought of her long blonde hair and knew he just had to do it no matter what anybody said.

"Why do we always have to come out here?" Sheri

complained, hugging her knees as she leaned against Mick. Peter took a beer can from his bag at his feet and pulled open the top. His dad always kept beer in the fridge and Peter had taken as many cans as he dared and shoved them into his knapsack. He prayed Mick had forgotten about the initiation but his hopes were soon dashed.

"Well, little boy, you all set for tonight?"

The others laughed softly, nudging each other. Peter didn't have to see them, he knew they were laughing, knew they thought he would back out. Part of him wanted to run home for a cup of tea and a warm bed. Instead, he took a deep breath and stared the older boy in the eyes. "I'm ready."

"There's all kinds of weird things in the forest."

"So what?"

Laughing, Mick looked around at the gang. "He don't believe me." Belching loudly, he crunched his empty beer can and threw it into the cemetery. Sheri grimaced.

That's right, Peter thought, he's a pig. Stay with me baby and I'll treat you right. He watched Mick's hand move up her thigh to her skirt then slip under it. She quickly pushed him away crossing her legs. "Not here," she whispered.

He smiled. "I'm just keeping my hand warm baby."

She pushed his hand away again. Jumping off the

wall Mick glared at her then moved to Peter. "When I say there are weird things here you should believe me Petey cause I'm out more than you are. Every night you go to your little middle class house with your little middle class boring parents. I stay out. I've slept out, here."

Alf rose, looking steadily at Peter. "We all have. To be part of the gang you got to rough it. No cosy little council houses or nuffink."

Mick grabbed a beer from Pete's bag and tore open the top. "When night comes you can feel the forest change."

Pete swallowed as Alf drew closer. "That's when things get really strange."

"Wha...." Pete stammered, rising to his feet, leaning against a tombstone.

Mick shoved his face inches from Pete's. "The pond, the Old Mill Ruins..."

"Baker's Hill," Alf cut in.

Mick stepped closer.

"At night they change into stinking, scary places."

"Perverts," Alf said, moving close to Pete and slowly, deliberately pulling a beer from his bag his eyes moving from one to the other.

"Murderers," Scobie whispered, stepping forward, forming a semi-circle around Pete.

"Rapists" Mick growled, glancing quickly at Sheri

then back to Pete.

His heart pounding, his mouth dry, Peter suddenly pushed through them then turned, taking deep breaths. "I don't believe you."

Mick sucked on his can as the beer flowed down his throat wiped his face and scowled. "It's no place for little boys. I don't think he's going to do it, do you?" Looking at the others, they all shook their heads, except Sheri, who simply stared at her shoes.

"He won't do it." Alf moved closer.

"Not a chance." Scobie said.

Puffing up his chest, Peter stepped back as they advanced on him and pointed a finger at Mick. "The questions is Mick, not if I have the balls to do it because I do, but if you have the balls to come and watch me do it."

Turning, he strode quickly away into the forest, leaving Mick dumbstruck behind him. The soft voice of Sheri drifted back to him through the forest and he smiled. "He really got you Mick," he heard her say.

Walking along the path, the forest seemed to move with strange life as if reaching out for him the branches closer than normal, the nettles more menacing than ever. Suddenly frightened he broke into a run until he was on the pavement and heading for home.

At midnight, they gathered by the Church, Alf and Scobie,

each carrying sticks with rags soaked in oil. Peter glanced at the gang around him, fear gnawing his insides. His stomach tight, his throat dry. Remember, why you are doing this, he thought. To get close to Sheri, the goddess of his life.

Only Mick and Sheri were missing.

"I should've known," Peter hissed. "He talks a good game but can't play it himself." He began to walk away towards the woods.

"Hey, Pete!" Alf stepped forward. "Where're you going?"

"To get it over with," he said over his shoulder.

"Wait!" Suddenly Mick appeared from the gloom in front of him, with Sheri in tow. Facing Pete, he unzipped his jacket, pulling a small bottle of scotch from his pocket. "It isn't midnight yet, little boy. Ten minutes to go."

"What difference does it make?"

Laughing, Mick helped Sheri up onto the wall, passing the bottle to her. No skirts, this time, Pete thought, just jeans and an old jacket to keep out the cold. His heart skipped. Even in jeans her figure was so delectable. He could feel his need for her, his frustration and could not take his eyes off her until Mick stepped in front of him, offering him the bottle. "It's a cold night. You're gonna need this, Petey."

God, the taste was awful! But he would not spit it

out instead he swallowed. He felt the warm liquid roll down his dry throat and momentarily settle his stomach. Lighting a cigarette Mick glanced at Pete through the smoke. "You can still pull out, if you want to." He smiled. "And be the wimp you truly are."

Handing the bottle back to Mick, Pete stared at the older boy. "I'm not backing out; but will you be there in the dark, waiting for me or you will be too scared and run."

Suddenly Mick raised his hand to hit Peter then looked at the others. In the gloom he could see contempt in their faces as Alf quickly stepped in front of him grabbing his hand. "This is a waste of time, Mick."

Nodding, Mick stepped back and put his bottle away. "Let's do it."

One by one the torches were lit, the flames casting eerie shadows as they moved through the forest.

In time, they reached a small clearing, which was surrounded by thick underbrush of stinging nettles. In the dancing light from the torches they could see that the path veered off to the right while to the left was an opening, like a cave, in the nettles with black, inky, darkness beyond.

Mick motioned to the opening. "In there," he said. "There's an old, dead trunk, about ten feet high. All you gotta do is climb it and shout the motto then come back. We'll know you've done it when we hear you shout so you'd better be loud. You have to be naked."

"I know. You said so before."

Looking around at the others, Peter's gaze fell on Sheri. Moving to her, he whispered. "Will you wait for me?"

Gently, she kissed his cheek and smiled. "We'll all be here. Good Luck, Pete."

Her perfume, her softness, the touch of her lips sent shivers of delight tearing through him, like electricity warming every part of him, helping to control his fear.

He searched her eyes. "Promise?" he said fearfully, afraid she might say no.

"I promise." She put her hands on his shoulder smiling.

"This is all very cozy..." Mick quickly pulled Sheri away, his arm around her and kissed her hard, then faced Pete. "It's time to become a man or stay a little boy. Who knows what things might be lurking in there. Things you can't even dream of in your worst night-mares." He shook his head, his arm around Sheri. "I don't think you can do it, little boy."

Stripping off his clothes, Pete spoke through gritted teeth. "Just make sure you're here when I come back."

Naked, he turned, plunging through the opening, into the darkness. Nettles stung his arms, hands and entire body as he held them over his face. Pain shot through his foot as dried and fallen thorns jabbed his sensitive skin. Still, he pushed on, the cold creeping over him, slowing him down.

The opening narrowed quickly, forcing him to crawl nettles scratching and digging into his back and thighs. More than ever he wished he was in his bed, asleep, telling himself over and over how stupid the whole thing was. Warm liquid ran down his back and legs. Blood. The going was slow and hard on his knees, which were now also bleeding.   Where the hell is the tree, he thought?

Blinded by the darkness and the thick blanket of nettles he pushed on. Suddenly, the ground under his knees and hands was moist, slimy and seemed to move as he moved. The stink of rotting vegetation was so powerful it made him choke and wretch. Surely, the tree must be somewhere.

Suddenly, he hit his forehead against something hard. Running his hands over the object, he felt the bark, the round trunk and slowly stood up, his hands going up the sides of the old tree. Though hard, it seemed to move under his touch while the wind's low moan pushed the nettles hard against him, biting deep into his flesh, the trees swaying under its increasing force.

Circling slowly around the tree, he found a branch sticking out from the old trunk at the perfect height for his foot. Moving his other hand above him, he suddenly felt another branch in the right place as if it had appeared just for him. Grabbing it, he began to climb, each time, finding a branch to hold just at the right moment. As he climbed the tree shuddered under him as if swayed by the wind.

A low eerie moan filled his ears. Not the wind this time but it seemed to come from the Tree! Alarm bells rang in his mind. Refusing to succumb he kept climbing. He would prove to Mick he was stronger and tougher. He prove to Sheri he was worthy of her attentions and he would prove to himself he was not afraid.

Reaching the top of the tree it was slimy and covered with a stinking, moss-like substance. Pulling himself onto the slippery top, he rested breathing heavily. Another moan seemed to roll out from the tree underneath him as though coming alive. It shook and shuddered. It's the wind, the wind only. He thought. Cold clutched every part of him. Needles of rain suddenly began to fall on his numb skin, making things worse. "I will not run, not run until this is done." He chanted. "I will not run till this is done."

Slowly standing, his feet sank into the ooze of the tree as it moved and shook under him. Precariously balanced, sliding on the slippery muck, fear shot through him. His voice croaked into a whisper. "Warriors...."

No. Yell it out, yell it out, so they could hear him and get it over with. Beneath his feet the tree shook and swayed, a deep moan emanating from inside it.

As fast as he could Peter shouted. "Warriors Rule!

Warriors Rule!"

Suddenly, the tree shook violently, as if trying to throw him off. Falling to his knees he slipped on the slime, grabbing a branch that melted away in his grip. The shaking, moaning tree now moved as if trying to uproot itself. It's only the wind. Just the wind.

Clutching for a handhold, he kept coming away with fistfuls of slimy muck as the branches cracked and slipped away from him. The tree shook hard. He could not keep his balance. The violent vibrating threw him into the air hitting an overhanging branch and falling into the nettles.

Crashing down through the thorns, cutting his arms and legs, he landed heavily on the moist ground. Filled with horror he watched the earth split apart as the tree's old roots pushed up towards him. Not the wind after all but something different, something terrible.

He had a sudden feeling as if he had disturbed something centuries old, that something, possibly the tree itself, was angry at his presence.

Standing up, he crashed through the underbrush as fast as he could towards the clearing. Behind, he could hear tearing and ripping as the tree's roots smashed through the earth seeking him.

Moments later he fell into the clearing blood-soaked and wild, his face gripped in fear. Mick stepped in front of him, grabbing his shoulders. "Hey Petey, what happened to you?"

"I'm part of the gang, now. Didn't you hear me? I did it. I'm in the gang now." Pete's wild eyes stared at the group standing around. Snatches of conversation came to him,

"Been gone a long time....looks bad..." None of it made sense.

Mick was laughing. "I didn't think you'd go through with it."

"Part of the gang now....."

Laughing Mick shook his head. "No you're not. It was a joke Petey. There is no initiation. You only become part of the gang if I say so. And I don't."

Mick's laughing face floated in his gaze. Anger suddenly shot through him.

"You bastard," Pete shouted. Spinning, he slammed his fist into Mick's face sending the older boy onto the ground.

Sheri fell to Mick's side, shaking his shoulders. Angrily she looked up at Pete. "It was just a joke. Can't you take a joke!"

"Yeah, look at me laughing."

Suddenly the roar from the trees made them all look up. The ground seemed to rip and tear as tentacles of nettles and roots snaked over the ground searching for them.

Pete turned to the others. "Pick up Mick and take him out of here."

They stared at the rippling ground, dumbstruck.

"Now!" Peter shouted. He pushed Alf and Scobie towards Mick. "Get going."

Sheri screamed. Peter threw on his trousers, then roughly gripped Sheri's arm as she screamed.

The earth erupted as old, slimly, stinking roots came towards them, wrapping around Mick's ankle. Quickly Pete picked up Mick's whiskey bottle, smashed it on a rock and began hammering the clinging vines. Looking at the others he shouted. "RUN!"

Tearing the stinking root from Mick's ankle, Pete grabbed one arm as Alf grabbed the other, dragging Mick after the others through the forest, the earth exploding with slithering tentacles expanding in all directions behind them. Pushing through the forest, in the gloom ahead stood the Church. Heading quickly for it, they pushed inside and slammed the door shut, Peter bolting it.

Stepping back from the door, they listened to the slithering, hissing, spitting roots enveloping the Church.

"What the hell is it?" Alf stared wild-eyed at Pete.

"The tree is alive. Like one of Mick's nightmares."

"We're going to die,"Scobie whimpered, the Church groaning under the weight of the tentacles as they wrapped around the building. "We're going to die," He cried.

"We're not going to die." Peter stared at them. "Some gang you are. Not so tough after all."

"What are we going to do," Alf whispered, swallowing hard.

Moving to the rows of pews Peter looked at the others. "We're in a Church aren't we? We're safe in a Church. We'll wait until morning."

Under the groaning beams, the slippery, crawling roots covering the building, banging against the doors and windows, they waited as the Church seemed to be slowly coming apart. Huddled together, they all silently prayed for morning.

Hours later, bright, brilliant sunshine of early morning, flowed through the stained glass windows of the old Church. The sounds and groans of the night before had gone giving way to the sounds of dawn, birds singing, gentle wind sifting through the now quiet trees. Unbolting the door, Pete threw it open, letting the morning light flood in. He looked back at the others now crowding around him.

"I'm glad I'm awake," Alf sighed. "It was just a dream, after all."

Shaking his head, Peter pointed to the ground outside the Church, torn and ripped from the roots that now lay dead under the morning sun. "It was no dream." He felt full of life and confident. One by one, he looked at the timid faces of the others, then stepped into the sunlight. Glancing back at the huddled group he sniffed. "I don't want to be part of your gang anyway. It's a waste of a life. I have better things to do with mine."

Then he strolled away into the sunlit forest towards home.

Sheri watched him go, while the others looked away.

Projector

Constable Wainwright stamped his cold feet again and looked at his watch. Only ten minutes had gone since he last looked.

Beating his hands together against the cold, he brought them up to his mouth and blew on them, trying to warm them up and looked out into the night. Pitch black. Freezing cold. Somewhere out there, quite near, was the lake; but he couldn't see it. There was no ambient light, for the sky was overcast. He'd been told that when there were no clouds, the sky was lit up like a Christmas tree by all the stars in the night sky. There were none tonight.

There were no lights of any description. Not like in the city where there were lights from buildings, cars, street lamps. There was nothing, except for the dim light coming through the curtains across the sliding doors that led into the chalet.

There could have been lights, he thought bitterly. There could have been a stove to keep warm; but the Inspector figured that his men should get their eyes used to the darkness so they could see movement in it. Having the lights blazing meant that beyond the range of it they would see nothing until it was too late. This way, with no lights, his men and whoever might attack them, were on equal ground. Wainwright knew there was a kind of logic to the inspector's thinking; but he didn't like it.

It wasn't just the darkness that made him uneasy it was also the noise; or the lack of it. There was nothing but the wind gently sighing through the trees all around him. Each time a branch touched another, he thought it was something else, something sinister. "It's only the wind," he would whisper to himself. It was definitely the noise he didn't like. No traffic, no talking, no music, none of the general noises of the city, just the wind.

He liked the city, any city; but London was his home. Being a policeman in London was a tough and dangerous job; but being out here in the middle of nowhere, with nobody around for miles, with no light except that of the light through the curtains, and in the middle of winter, scared him. It was eerie, he thought, almost unreal.

But being on a special assignment, protecting a witness from a group of deadly fanatics, scared him more. He was on the outside, guarding the place. If anything did happen he would be the first to get hit. Yes, he was definitely scared.

He looked at his watch again. Time for another round.

Suddenly he stopped, listening hard. A low mournful howl drifted to him from out of the darkness. Then another howl answered it. Wolves! In the briefing, they'd been told there were wolves around here; but he'd never expected to see or hear them. More howls drifted to him. They were far away, perhaps on the other side of the lake. "Poor sods," he thought. At least when his shift was over he could go into a nice warm chalet; but they would have to stay outside in the deep cold.

From the rusted table beside him, he picked up his automatic rifle, switched off the safety catch and swung the strap over his shoulder so that the gun lay across his chest. Also from the table, he picked up his powerful torch and clicked it onto its housing on top of the rifle. Switching it on, its powerful yellow beam knifed into the darkness.

With one hand holding the barrel grip and his other on the trigger, Wainwright began a slow, methodical, sweep around the entire chalet, swinging the beam of the torch over the structure, over trees, stumps, at the wood pile, between parked vehicles, at the utility sheds, at the basement windows, over the narrow patch of land between the chalet and the wooden stairs leading down to the boat house and dock. Everything was covered with a think layer of frost that crunched underfoot with every step he took. Like the patrol of an hour before, it was uneventful.

When he returned to the table on the porch at the rear of the chalet, he heard it. Just as he laid the rifle down on the table he heard it. A faint, thudding, beating noise that came up from the dock, almost inaudible; but it was there.

The chalet sat on the edge of a precipice with only a few feet of grass separating the porch from the cliff edge. The porch ran the length of the rear of the building with a railing all the way around it, except for one end, the stairs that curved down the cliff to the boathouse end. It had a sloping roof held up by pillars on each corner of the railing and two in the middle. During the summer months, windows with screens were inserted in the gaps between the railing and the porch roof; but they'd been taken out on the Inspector's orders. He claimed it would make seeing in the dark much easier and besides, the glass wouldn't stop a bullet.

The sound came again. Louder this time. Thud, thud, wumph, wumph.

Unclipping the torch from its holder on the automatic rifle, Wainwright stepped off the porch and stood at the top of the stairs playing the beam over the wooden steps down to the boathouse below; but he saw nothing unusual. Fear gnawed at his stomach. Turning away from the stairs he slowly ran the beam over the woods several yards away from the chalet, trying to squint into the darkness looking for movement; but he saw nothing.

He was acutely aware that he was away from his weapon, even though it was only a few feet away. Then he heard it again.

Suddenly, he looked up and it came at him right of the darkness. He shrieked. As he stumbled backwards, the torch fell from his hand, bounced off the top step and disappeared over the edge.

Ripping and tearing suddenly filled the night and the last sound that Wainwright heard before he was torn to pieces was a rush of air as if something was inhaling. After a few seconds the sounds abruptly ceased and the thud, thud, wumph, wumph, faded away.

Only the faint mournful howl of a wolf broke the restored stillness of the night.

She rolled off the bed and stared out of the upstairs window that looked out onto the rear of the chalet and the scenic views of the lake. From her bedroom window she would have been able to see the boathouse and the dock below; but all the lights outside were off so all she saw was darkness.

But she'd heard the noise. Even over the sounds of the television and voices coming from the living room downstairs, she'd heard the noise.

Rolling back onto the bed, she grabbed her iPad from the bedside table. Running her fingers deftly over it she looked at the area map showing the location of everybody nearby, represented by small circles. They all glowed white except for one that glowed red. A small smile crossed her lips.

Detective Sergeant Baxter yawned and stretched in his chair. Across from him, Constable Payne stared morosely at the meager pile of poker chips at his end of the table and the large pile on Baxter's end. Payne was losing and he didn't like losing, especially to Baxter. He was sure the DS was cheating; but he couldn't figure out how. The man was too smug to start with. Baxter had this habit of talking down to everyone, just because he'd been in Iraq. He was always telling everyone that He was the weapons specialist. Well, Payne was explosives; but Baxter always spoke condescendingly to him. If he could just prove that Baxter was cheating! Pretending to yawn and stretch like that he's not even concentrating. Trying to throw me off, thought Payne. He knew it was a bluff.

Payne laid his cards down triumphantly. "Three Jacks. Beat that!'

Baxter smiled widely, "No problem." Four aces went down, face up.

He'd won again.

"How the hell did you do that?"

Baxter smiled his toothy grin at Payne. "My night, mate."

"I've had enough of this," Payne slammed his cards on the table. "I'll get you back somehow, sir. I think you're cheating!"

"That's a pretty bad accusation, constable, I hope you can prove it."

"I can't. You know damn well know I can't," Payne said, throwing back his chair and angrily pointing his finger at Baxter. "But I'll never play with you again."

Payne ran down the spiral staircase with short quick steps and slammed the front door behind him.

Chuckling, Baxter began to clear the table, pulling the pile of money towards him, then stopped as another voice drifted up to him from the living room below.

"We're a team Sergeant. We can't afford division. Let him win next time."

Baxter glanced through the railing down at Chief Inspector Ryan. A strong, powerfully built man. Stretched out on the sofa, reading the paper, relaxed Baxter could see the man's authority, strength – like a coiled tiger ready to spring.

"Chief, the man's a nob…"

"So are you, Sergeant."

"He deserves…."

"I'm not asking, Baxter."

An iPad on the coffee table beside Ryan suddenly burst into life, chiming loudly before Baxter could reply to his boss.

"That'll be London," said Ryan, as he picked up the

tablet pressing the switch. The screen suddenly came to life, illuminating the face of his superior, Superintendent Alice Cummings. "Ma'am"

"Jimmy. Good to see you. How are things there?"

"All secure this end, Ma'am."

"Good. And how's our guest? Any problems?"

Ryan shook his head. "No, all quiet."

Cummings nodded. "Listen Jimmy, we've had some intelligence that the rest of the cult are planning something, but as of yet we don't know what. Knowing them, it will be nasty."

"I thought they were on the run."

"So did we, but it seems they have regrouped without the Professor and are getting back to their old games. We've been watching one or two and there is something going on so keep your eyes peeled. With the technology the Professor had their reach could extend far beyond London."

Ryan looked at the woman on the screen. "Is there a serious threat?"

"We're not sure Jimmy, as of yet, but it is shaping up to look that way. I must dash. The Commissioner is wetting himself over this. Speak soon." With that the screen went dead. Ryan sat in contemplation for a moment when Baxter piped up.

"It doesn't sound too good, boss."

Ryan looked up at the Sergeant. "No. But we're miles away, so probably nothing will happen," he then thought about that for a moment. "But let's keep an eye out, just in case."

"Will do…."

The Sergeant's words were suddenly cut off as the sliding doors at the end of the living room flew open and Payne came in quickly, out of breath. "Wainwright's gone."

"What?" Ryan was on his feet still holding the tablet, while the paper fell to the floor in a mess. "Any of the cars gone?"

"No, Sir."

"Then he must have gone after somebody in the woods."

"I don't think so, Chief. I think somebody went after him." Payne dropped Wainwright's automatic rifle on the chair beside the sofa. "I found that on the deck."

"What about his torch?"

Payne shrugged. "I can't find it. Chief, there was blood everywhere."

"Christ, it's starting." From the coffee table Ryan grabbed his nine millimetre automatic pistol and ammunition clip. He rammed the clip into the gun, clicked off the safety catch and then jammed the pistol into his shoulder holster.

From the loft level Baxter came down and joined

them carrying his automatic rifle. He quickly, expertly, checked it, making sure it was ready to fire.

Now was the test, thought Ryan. Men of experience putting themselves on the line to protect a key witness from a group of dangerous fanatics who would stop at nothing to make sure she couldn't testify against the Professor. Ryan hoped that justice would have time to be served.

To Baxter, he said. "Sergeant, slip out the front, stay under cover and keep moving. Wait until the last minute before you fire and conserve your ammunition."

As Baxter left, Ryan turned to Payne. "Go wake up Burns and Cassidy," he said. "Tell Burns I want him upstairs in the hall, lights off, by the window. And tell him to keep her locked in no matter what. Send Cassidy out the back and under the deck. You station yourself down here in the master bedroom, lights off."

"Sir."

Payne slipped away quietly as Ryan switched off the lamp on the table beside the sofa, plunging the living room into darkness. He moved into the kitchen as he heard Payne softly run upstairs to the bedrooms in the loft above. He moved to the window, peering into the gloom. His heart was pumping, hard, his gun at his side.

In the loft upstairs was the open den area where Baxter and Payne had played cards. Off this ran a hallway with three bedrooms and a bathroom. Ryan knew that Burns would be at the end of the hallway, by the window, in the darkness. Outside, he knew Cassidy would have positioned himself under the deck to give anyone trying to get in through the sliding doors a nasty surprise. Payne would be in the master bedroom, off the living room, at the window while Baxter, his wild card, an ex-Special Forces man, would be circling, ready to strike, somewhere out there in the night.

Ryan was confident they would be ok.

She sat on the bed because she didn't need to see outside. Everything was going according to plan. God bless the Professor, she thought. They thought they were protecting her from his followers; but they knew nothing. His plan, his vision, was well underway.

She shivered with pleasure, remembering his touch. Oh, how she longed for him. But this would be as sweet, she thought. What fools they were.

Holding the tablet in her hands, she touched another blip on the area map and the name flashed across the screen, the white blip flashing red.

Cassidy lay on the hard frozen dirt under the deck, his automatic rifle ready. He listened intently. No sound, save for the wind.

Suddenly, the wooden beam above his head creaked. He crawled sideways. Again the wooden beam above his head creaked and a soft hissing, beating noise floated to him.

He crawled forwards.

The board directly above him groaned heavily.

His throat was dry and he swallowed as this hissing grew louder. Fear gripped him. Frantic, he began crawling backwards, further under the deck.

Suddenly, a light pierced the darkness, blinding him. This hissing and beating was loud in his ears and he screamed as something came at him. But his scream was choked off by the sounds of hacking and gurgling. There was a sudden rush of air, and abruptly, the sounds ceased and the hissing died away.

On the bed she dreamed as the tablet flashed in her hand. She remembered the Professor. Long ago she'd discovered what happened when people defied Him. Even she had felt the brunt of His wrath. The scars on her thighs showed how cruel he could be; but then all disciples had to learn. She'd learned quickly and learned the rewards quickly: power, wealth, destruction of His enemies, a new order.

She imagined his tongue on her skin and let a tear roll down her cheek. They thought she was working for them! Idiots!

She pressed another white blip on the tablet screen and another name appeared.

Payne stood by the sliding doors with Ryan. "I swear I heard it, Chief."

"See anything?"

"No sir."

Ryan snapped on the outside lights, flooding the entire deck with bright white light. He saw the blood on the wooden beams of the deck which he presumed was Wainwright's; but there was no sign of Cassidy. Peering through the open sliding doors he saw no sign of movement, no sound except for the gentle wind. He called for Cassidy but got no reply. Switching off the outside lights he quickly shut the sliding doors and turned to Payne.

"What about the radio?"

Payne shook his head. "Static."

"Mobile?"

"No, sir."

"What about Baxter?"

Again, Payne shook his head. "Not answering radio or mobile."

"Shit."

Outside, Baxter circled slowly in the woods beyond the

chalet, keeping his gaze on the building. He'd heard something that he was sure came from the back. His finger rested gently on the trigger of his automatic rifle, as his senses tingled with excitement. Just like the war, he thought.

He reached the back of the chalet, just as Ryan turned off the outside lights.

Crouched low just by the tree line, he heard a faint humming, whirring and beating. It was somewhere above him. Suddenly the noise grew louder as if coming towards him. Baxter turned and disappeared into the woods.

Her body tingled. Soon it would be done and in the morning she would rendezvous with the others to begin the second phase of His plan. Even though He was miles away, she knew that He approved. God, how she missed Him, needed Him.

Burns knew something was terribly wrong.

He stood at the end of the hall by the window staring into the gloom. Over the last few minutes he'd heard some odd sounds, strange muffled beating and whirring sounds. He'd also heard the faint voices of Payne and Ryan talking downstairs. There were two bedrooms on one side of the hall and a bathroom and bedroom on the other. Save for the bathroom the three bedrooms were locked.

Burns didn't mind babysitting witnesses especially if it meant that criminals would be put away then he was all for it. Very rarely dangerous, this type of work was usually dull and boring. But this was much different. Fanatics would kill at the drop of a hat for their cause. There was no reasoning with them. The cultists they were protecting her from were the worst he'd ever run across.

Taking out a set of keys, Burns moved down the hall, checking each of the bedrooms, locking them behind him. He stopped outside her room, unlocked the door and pushed it open with the muzzle of his gun. Expecting to see her sleeping he was stunned when It rushed at him from out of the darkness.

Pain burst over him and he tried to cry out but the hacking, eviscerating and whirring sounds muffled any screams he could make.

Downstairs, Ryan froze, hearing the noises. A second later glass exploded and he was sprinting up the stairs to the end of the hall.

The window had been smashed apart leaving a gaping hole. Burns' rifle lay on the floor and blood covered one wall. There was no sign of Burns himself.

The woman!

Ryan burst into her room only to find it empty, that she too had gone.

Another scream pierced the night, sending shivers down his spine. "Payne!"

Chopping and whirring answered him. There was a sudden rush of air and then silence.

Ryan ran downstairs shouting. "Payne! Payne, where the hell are you?"

Searching the living room and the downstairs bedroom, he found no sign of his officer except for the blood that covered the sliding doors. Returning to the hallway upstairs, he picked up Burns rifle, pulled out the clip, saw that it was full and rammed it home. The safety catch was off and he was ready. His heart pumped hard and he could feel his adrenalin coursing through him. Ryan was scared; but he knew how to use his fear to his advantage. Fear kept him sharp, alert, strong.

Suddenly the whirring came from right outside the shattered window. What the hell was he dealing with? Ryan ran down the hall towards the stairs, the noise just above and behind him.

Pounding down the stairs he missed a step and fell, rolling hard the noise almost on top of him. At the bottom of the stairs he swivelled and pulled the trigger; but it had moved off before he could hit it.

Up again, he ran to the sliding doors, turned and fired two more blasts as he crashed through onto the deck outside. It was almost on top of him.

Shattering the stillness of the night he fired again at point blank range. The whirring and beating changed to a deeper, rougher note and its spinning jaws vibrated a little harder.

But it was no use. It came at him relentlessly, cutting him, hacking at him, disintegrating him, absorbing him, his screams lost over the whirring, beating sounds and, as always, it quickly died away.

She felt wonderful. Projector had done its work.

Her body soaked with perspiration, she felt light-headed and tired, but fully satiated. The police had paid dearly for their part in capturing the Professor. They thought that by cutting off the head of the movement, the movement would die. They were wrong. Planting her as a witness, promising to deliver all the names of the cult members was a stroke of genius and a perfect way to exact revenge. By pretending to betray the cult she had been placed in a perfect position to complete the first phase, letting them know that the movement was still strong and powerful.

How sweet the revenge was. She went to bed remembering His kisses, His words, one world, one people together under His philosophy.

In the morning, she packed her bag and went downstairs to make breakfast. After such a deep sleep and the events of the night before she was very hungry. Another person would have run from the scene of carnage; but she decided she must stay. It gave her strength.

Sipping her coffee she thought about the Professor and their love. His charisma still filled her, His kisses still made her body tingle. She couldn't wait to see Him again. She remembered every part of Him, his piercing eyes, tall frame and shock of white hair were his most prominent features.

Together, they'd built the perfect killing machine, Projector.

The Army wanted a machine that was small, flew like a helicopter, was almost silent and could tear someone to bits, suck up all the remains for fuel then proceed on its way. It was really quite easy. Using existing Unmanned Aerial Vehicle technology they'd built and refined their creation.

The Professor soon realized that no government could have his machine. Only He, its creator, could us it. First to destroy all those who stood in the way of His vision, then to guard His vision and His followers. All governments would disappear and only one world, one people and one order, His order, would remain.

She thought about how the government people and police had tried to stop them by destroying the lab and capturing the Professor. Imbeciles! She'd helped him create the machine, she knew how to use it too! Now in a few minutes when the others arrived, phase two would begin.

Suddenly, the tablet on the bed beeped.

Glancing at it, she went cold. The area map on the screen showed a single flashing red blip, which she knew was her. Then she heard it. A beating, whirring, wumph, wumph, just outside the window.

She tapped the screen furiously trying to type in the termination code; but there was no response. The red dot continued to flash.

Suddenly a letter appeared on the screen, the first letter of her name. Again, she tried to type in the code. Nothing.

The second letter appeared. She could see it through the window, its spinning, snapping jaws mocking her. My God, she thought, it's re-programming itself.

The third letter flashed onto the screen. Paralyzed by fear, she couldn't move. The last letter showed and her name began to flash.

Outside the window it was waiting for her, mocking her as if it had a mind of its own.

Had it been damaged by Ryan's bullets? She thought the whirring sounded rougher, its vibrations much deeper and coarser than before. Perhaps that was it? Her name flashed on the screen. Her mind raced as she tried to figure a way out.

She swallowed.

"Oh God. No," she whispered.

Suddenly, the window shattered and she screamed.

Outside Baxter stepped out from behind a tree and stood in the clearing between the chalet and the woods. He looked at the screen of his mobile phone and the red blip that was now constant. As the thrashing, whirring and beating noises died away he watched the red blip disappear.

Hearing the sounds of people coming through the woods, he turned and raised his gun. Three figures emerged from the trees, all dressed in black. They joined him. Baxter lowered his gun.

"Well?" The first man said to Baxter.

"Taken care of, " Baxter replied. "And the Professor?"

"Also taken care of. Along with the rest of the cult."

Baxter nodded. "Projector?"

"Two and four. The first blew itself up."

"Good."

"And this one," said one of the other figures.

"It was damaged. I sent it to the bottom of the lake."

"Excellent. Whitehall will be pleased. Let's go."

Together the four men left the clearing and headed

97

back into the woods towards a waiting vehicle some distance away.

For a long time there was silence, save for the sound of the wind through the trees, then suddenly there was the sound of a splash from the lake and faint sounds of whirring and beating that slowly drifted away to silence.

Roadhogs

It was late when Locke pulled off the M11 onto a quiet road towards home. "We cannot possibly justify a rise for you at this time." The words rolled around his head. At this time? What the hell did that mean?

Rain danced on the windshield. How long do you wait before they notice you, he thought.

Tyres gripped the wet pavement as the car twisted and turned. Corrupt politicians, crime going up, everybody looking after number one. Yes, he thought, nice guys definitely finish last.

Ahead the tail-lights of another car disappeared around the corner.

The rain fell harder, cutting down visibility.

He felt used. His ideas lost on his plodding boss. God, given the chance his designs could make things better, he knew it.

Suddenly, a Ford Estate wagon pulled out of an intersection directly in front of him.
Idiot!

Frantic, Locke hit the brakes skidding the car sideways. Wrenching the wheels right, then left, he quickly straightened out. Furious, Locke shook his fist, but the other car sped away. He could have been killed. Sweat poured down his body, his heart pumping as he pulled onto the side of the road. A pair of headlights swept past him.

Later, he pulled his white BMW into the driveway of his home, a detached, modest brick house in a quiet suburban area of Epping. Surrounded by overgrown hedgerows with wild roses flowering amongst the paving stones, his house looked as if it too had been planted, growing out of the earth like all the vegetation around it. Ivy framed the doorway, covering the brick and woodwork. Like walking into cosy cottage. His wife had made their home warm and comfortable.

He felt numb from shock as he walked to his door. Driven off the road by a maniac! He still could not believe it. Thank God the car still ran!

Unlocking the door, Locke stepped inside. Sanctuary.

At the end of the street a pair of headlights turned into the road, slowed and stopped.

Locke sat bolt upright, eyes wide open, breathing hard. The bedroom. Sweat trickled down his body, the bed damp.

Quiet seeped through the house. Outside, wind rustled the trees and light drifted through the window from the streetlamp. She lay beside him asleep. Visions of the estate wagon standing alone, its doors gaping open blackness beyond, a huge dark room, men screaming, still

101

clung to him. Another sleepless night.

"You didn't sleep."

"No," Locke said sitting down at the kitchen table. Toast appeared in front of him brought by Sarah, his wife.

He looked at her. Small, petite, cute and pretty with wide inquisitive eyes and a smile that electrified any room she walked into, Sarah was his anchor, his rock. "Darling, are you worried about something? Is it work?"

He shook his head. "No." He was late. Getting up this morning had been difficult. His eyes were scratchy from fatigue. "We'll talk about it later."

Before she could reply he kissed her quickly, saying, "I love you. I'll see you tonight. Have a good day, sweetheart."

With that he was gone, the door shutting behind him.

Drizzle from the lowering grey skies soaked the car as he drove over the twisting road towards the motorway. Another corner. Hedgerows on both sides made each curve blind. Tail-lights occasionally peaked through the thick brush far ahead of him. The wipers leapt across the windshield and dropped back into their sockets.

Ahead, the intersection where the Ford suddenly appeared the night before shot past, now empty. No car came shooting forward. In a few miles he would reach the morning traffic. Glancing in his mirror, he was suddenly afraid.

It couldn't be. Coming up fast behind him came the Ford. It was going to run him the Ford sat off his bumper, its lights flashing.

Gripping the steering wheel, Locke steered through hard curves and short straights. This way. That way. Faster and faster. The Ford right on his tail! The front tyre grazed the grass verge.

The wheel danced in his grip. He gulped. Suddenly, the Ford pulled out shooting past him. Metal screeched against metal! The Ford's rear grazed the BMW forcing Locke to brake fast.

The estate car shot ahead, then, inexplicably stopped dead in the road. God! Locke jammed the brakes, the wheels locking, pulling up inches from the Ford's bumper. Blood rushed into his head from his pounding heart.

An engine gunned and the estate wagon roared away leaving the BMW in its mist. "Christ!" Locke hammered the steering wheel in frustration. Not again, it couldn't happen again.

Sir Maynard Taylor, lit his pipe as he paced around the cramped office. "Well," he coughed, his belly shaking. "Well." His hacking over, he glared at Locke. "Did you get a look at the man?"

"No, we were travelling too fast, Sir."

"Too fast! Too fast! That's no excuse." He thrust the stem of his pipe at Locke. "You didn't get the license number I suppose?"

"No."

"No of course not. That's too much to ask!" The pipe rolled round and round in Sir Maynard's hand, his agitation growing. Jamming it between his teeth, he resumed his pacing. Years of enjoying the perks of being a senior civil servant, the drink, the richest foods, the parties into the small hours, cavorting with the rich and famous, plenty of young woman seeking to be in the company of the powerful, had made him flabby and soft. Those were the days, he thought. Now where was he? Retired from the civil service, a director in a corporation that dealt with information technology – something he knew nothing about and, worse still, investigated for alleged sexual misconduct with some of those same young women he'd cavorted with in his younger days, who, as far as he was concerned, were out to make as much money off him as they could. It was an outrage he thought. You couldn't trust anyone these days. His portly belly rolled and jiggled as he moved as Locke's voice suddenly broke his reverie.

"You're not supposed to smoke in here, Sir."

"What? I'll smoke where I damn well like."

Locke was silent for a few minutes as the big man continued to pace. Then he said. "They were probably just hooligans, Sir Maynard."

"Hooligans? Hooligans? Are they hooligans who know where you live, where you work? Doesn't sound like hooligans to me. If anything happened it would be a disaster of unparalleled proportion. We can't have your designs going to the highest bidder can we? If only one of these pip-squeak countries, or worse terrorist groups, got hold of your reality technology, it would be a catastrophe!"

"What kind of car was it?"

For the first time Locke turned to Higgins, head of security. His military bearing confident, quiet air and cold blue eyes gave him a powerful menacing presence. Those who feared him called him The Ghost, because he seemed to appear and disappear so quickly and silently down the corridors of SDT Corporation, their employer.

"A grey Ford Estate," Locke replied. Glancing at Sir Maynard, he continued. "What do I do if it happens again?"

"Do? Do?" Maynard stopped pacing, leaning his bulk on the cluttered desk. "I'll tell you what you do. You get away. Drive off, and go straight to the police. Let them handle it. It's got to be nipped in the butt, nipped in the butt, yes?"

"I think the word you're looking for is bud, Sir Maynard, nipped in the bud," Higgins said drily.

Maynard shot him an angry glance, then thumped the desk. "Nipped in the bud, Locke!" With a sudden flurry of activity, Sir Maynard left the office, Higgins right behind him, who silently closed the door, leaving Locke on his own dreading the end of the working day.

Tail-lights gleamed far ahead through the trees as he drove. Glimpses of red in the evening's gathering gloom made him feel melancholy. His hands sweated on the wheel, his clothes stuck to the seat. He glanced in his rear view mirror. The road behind him was clear. Sir Maynard's words floated in his head. Catastrophe, Disaster.

Trembling, he dreaded each curve, every corner, the strain growing by the minute. Why don't they come? Was the game over, he wondered? Was Higgins right? Were they just hooligans in a stolen car?

Shivers ran up and down his body, the fear making him feel sick, edgy, worn out and trapped. If nothing happened tonight there was always tomorrow, or the day after.

Home at last! Quickly turning off the engine he climbed out, slammed the car door and ran into the house as fast as his stumbling legs would carry him. At the end of the road headlights stabbed through the darkness as the Ford slowly pulled up across from his house.

"What about the police," she said.

Shrugging, Locke poured another cup of coffee, his hands trembling slightly. "What can they do? No crime has been committed."

Sarah brought a small tray of coffee and biscuits into the living room and watched her husband fall heavily onto the sofa, tired and worn out. He wasn't sleeping and this was his third coffee of the evening – very unusual for him.

Elegantly, she took an Arrowroot from the plate on the coffee table and sat down beside him. Crunching the biscuit she took his hand in hers. "Road rage is a crime. This person drove you off the road. The police have to get involved. What did your boss say?"

"Same as you, that I should go to the police but that's easier said than done. Everything happens so fast there's no time to pull over and run for help. The guy's gone before I even get out of the car!"

Sick at heart, he gulped the last of his coffee. A twitch under his left eyelid made him feel edgy. He squeezed Sarah's hand, thankful for her support. Nibbling on the Arrowroot, she squeezed him back. "There must be something you can do."

The next morning, Locke stood at the window of his office staring down at the car park in front of SDT's offices. Four floors up, he watched a man leaning against a blue sedan his face bent downward against the rain.

The car beside the man was a grey estate wagon. But was it the same one! Who was the man? Locke moved to the workbench and the row of computer monitors around his cluttered office. The man outside had been there 15 minutes. Locke had checked it carefully with his watch. Sitting down at his desk, opposite the workbench, he leaned for the phone.

"It isn't a matter of wasting valuable time, Locke. But did you get a good look at the fellow?" Sir Maynard paced back and forth in Locke's office gripping his pipe.

"His face was turned away from me," Locke replied.

"I see. Well we don't seem to be doing very well do we?"

"It doesn't matter, Andrew." Higgins purred softly, perched on the only other chair, giving Sir Maynard room to manoeuvre his bulk. "The man was long gone right after Mr Locke called me. The car too."

"Well, should we be worried, James? Could it have been one of your people?"

Higgins shook his head. "No, but I don't think this is anything to worry about." Glancing at Locke he smiled thinly. "But I'll have one of my men follow you tonight to make sure you get home safely."

Mozart filled the car, flowing over him from the finely tuned stereo as he drove home. He felt at ease for the first time in a long time, knowing that behind him Higgins' man followed.

The safety was bliss.

The road was quiet.

Suddenly a horn blared behind him! He jumped.

Headlights in his rear mirror weaved from side to side!

It was the Ford!

Shit! Where the hell was Higgin's man? He cursed inwardly. Gunning the engine, Locke pushed the BMW hard; but the Ford remained only a few feet from his rear bumper.

Around a curve! Down-shift fast! Tyres squealing, the wheel spinning in his hands.

Gripping it hard, he rammed the stick into fourth, hit the gas pedal and shot out of the curve. The Ford still sat right off his bumper, horn blaring. Another curve. Locke's wheels slipped badly. Too fast! Hitting the brakes, sweating, he fought to stay on the road.

Suddenly the Ford shot ahead, swerving into him.

He's trying to drive me off the road! Where the Hell is Higgins!

His tyres hit the grass verge.

The wheel spun in his hands. Locke hit the gas.

The BMW shot forward but the Ford came at him again, ramming his door. The wheel jumped and spun. He couldn't keep the car steady as the back swung out on the slippery road. Another curve. Too fast! Hit the brakes! Suddenly he was moving slower than the Ford that shot ahead of him.

I've had enough of this, he thought. Seeing his opportunity, Locke pumped the gas pedal and shot up beside the Ford and rammed its door. Quickly racing ahead he cut across in front, slicing the Ford's fender forcing it onto the grass. Ramming into the hedgerows it spun around in circles finally skidding into a ditch on the shoulder.

Locke jammed the brakes hard, his tyres screeching on the pavement. The BMW came to a rest sideways on the road. Jolted, Locke snapped back against the headrest, held in place by the shoulder harness.

Trembling, he slowly extricated himself from the stricken BMW, now a scarred and dented wreck.

With rain pouring down on him, he began shaking as he stood beside his car. The road was now deserted and quiet. The estate car lay half-hidden in the undergrowth, tangled in hedgerows and on its side in the ditch, the windshield cracked in web-like intricacy.

Slowly Locke approached the wrecked Ford. Gingerly, he bent down to look inside. Suddenly, quickly he stood up, stumbled, and fell back against the car, taking deep breaths. It couldn't be!

Sarah!

He looked again....

"No, that's the wrong ending." Locke threw down his headset. "I'll make it Sir Maynard." For it to work she needed an accomplice. Higgins maybe, he thought?

He needed a cigarette.

Moving to the window he glanced around his cramped office. The leading edge of real scenario information technology, far beyond contemporary gaming software, was here in this room and it was his invention, his baby. His software was so real that it was almost impossible to tell the reality from the fantasy. Everyone from the medical profession to the military desperately wanted his ideas.

It had been a long, hard struggle. Now, though, he was happy. Sitting down at his desk, he gulped down some cold coffee and resumed working, this time making Sir Maynard the baddie.

Hours later when Locke finished the programme he transferred all of his files to a USB stick. Then he wiped all the hard drives in his office making sure there was no trace of his work. The very thing the fool Maynard was worried about would be reality, Locke thought, chuckling to himself. Idiots. His ideas in unfriendly hands, put there by him, who, tomorrow, would be rich, the money for all his designs in his account.

Shutting off the machines, he put on his coat and walked out of SDT's offices for the last time and once outside, headed for his car; the grey Ford Estate parked beside Maynard's gleaming white BMW.

Locke's BMW was to be red.

He'd chosen it the previous day.

Split Second

Harper didn't see the car. It came quickly out of the drive. Tyres screeched on the wet pavement. Metal slammed against metal. Harper's bicycle flew out from under him and for a split second he hung motionless in the air then fell heavily onto the road.

Pain hammered up his back, his eyes blurring. He stared over at the bicycle only a few feet away, focusing his eyes intently on the still spinning back wheel.

Concentrate, concentrate. Somehow he felt that if he relaxed his concentration he would slip away. Voices slowly drifted to him as faces began crowding around him looking down on him.

"Oh my God, I didn't see him."

"Christ, he looks bad."

"Somebody call an ambulance."

He saw the sun's reflection on the screen of a mobile phone that someone put up to their ear; but he couldn't see all of it. He had to keep concentrating.

Silence.

The contrast was sudden, intense. The pain had gone but he was cold and damp. He still lay by the side of the road, the bicycle only a few feet away, its wheel turning. A little slower than before.

Where is everybody, he thought.

The faces that had crowded over him had gone.
The road was deserted.

Looking around, he noticed the car was behind him,
off the road, its front end pushed into the hedge, the doors
open.

His head felt woolly, almost numb as he slowly
stood up. Blood oozed down his cheek from a gash in his
forehead and suddenly the pain came back, this time with
dizziness as well. Staggering over to the car, he fell
against it and looked inside. Empty.

The keys were still in the ignition.

If I can get to a phone I'll be ok.

The car would be his best bet for getting help.
Climbing inside, he turned the keys; but the engine refused
to fire. Again and again he tried to start the car but without
success. Hitting the steering wheel angrily, stabbing
needles of pain shot into his head and then gradually died
away. Gingerly he climbed out of the car and looked up the
deserted road in both directions.

Which way?

He began walking unsteadily along the pavement.
A moment later, Harper stopped outside a set of locked iron
gates. Beyond he could see a vague outline of buildings
through the trees at the end of a winding drive. He
searched for an opening and found one a few feet from the

115

gates – small opening in the stone wall surrounding the grounds. Squeezing through it he headed up the drive towards a large manor house.

The drive ended in a square car park directly in front of an impressive entrance where stone steps led up to two large, heavy, wooden doors. Beyond, the landscaped grounds seemed to stretch on forever.

The sound of nearby laughter made him turn sharply. A couple strolled across the grass towards him. Harper called out to them. "Hello! Please, I need some help. I've been in an accident."

The couple walked right past him without seeing him or registering his existence. Stunned Harper stared after them. Could anybody really be so uncaring? What kind of people are they? Here I am in need of help, blood oozing from my forehead and they complete ignore me.

He watched them climb up the stone steps, unlock the large door and open it. If I could get inside I could at least lie down somewhere and soothe my head.

He followed them up the steps. "Wait!"

Neither of the two acknowledged his cry.

Slowly the large front door began to close as the couple entered the building. Harper slipped inside quickly.

A simple man, he was rarely impressed by anything. He liked to read books, for long walks and ride his bicycle in the beautiful country lanes and woods around

Salisbury. He spent a lot of time looking at wildlife through binoculars and photographing whatever species or specimens caught his interest. He would always buy his food from the green grocer and the butcher having vowed to never set foot in a supermarket. A loveless man, he believed he was safer being single. He didn't spend much money and he lived comfortably and in peace. But years of loneliness had hardened him to most things of beauty. Until now.

Now, he stood, open-mouthed in a large foyer replete with giant exotic tapestries. Huge portraits and ornate mirrors hung between the tapestries. And from the high ceilings two sparkling, beautiful, chandeliers gracefully spread like bursting fireworks from the pristine plaster.

Across the long, polished tile floor was a small lift while along the left wall a beautiful broad, plushly carpeted, staircase curved up the walls into the secrets of the house.

The heavy front door closed loudly behind him.

Startled, the man, Frank, stopped suddenly on the staircase and looked back at the doors where Harper stood.

"What is wrong with you people?" Harper pleaded.

"What's wrong, Frank." Carole stood a few steps above Frank, looking down at him.

"I thought I heard something."

Laughing softly, Carole came down a step. "Must

have been the wind. You're too tense, darling." She caressed his face playfully with both hands. "Mummy will take good care of you."

"Will Mummy wear that sexy little dress I like so much?"

"Anything for my boy."

Laughing, they kissed and arm in arm went up the stairs leaving Harper bewildered behind them.

What the hell is going on, he thought. He looked right at me; but didn't see me.

He stared after them.

They can't be deaf and they're not blind. So they must be mad!

Looking around the deserted foyer, Harper suddenly felt very alone. Something strange was happening to him that made no sense. Gripped by fear he quickly followed Frank and Carole up the stairs. The one thing he knew was that he had to be with people. If he could find someone with some sense then he could get help.

At the top of the staircase Harper saw Frank and Carole open a door with a number on it at the far end of a long hall and Harper realized they were going into a flat. He could see it was a self closing door so he hurried down the hall and stepped inside just before the door closed. Leaning against the wall his efforts left him aching and tired.

Harper drew in a breath. The flat was huge and beautiful. The ornate windows went from the floor up to the ceiling. It was completely open. The lounge and dining area were one large space. The kitchen too was open. A broad counter and cupboards separated it from the dining area. The kitchen was modern, fully equipped with the latest devices with light oak cupboards and pale blue tiles that reflected the sun that poured through the large window over the double sink.

Suddenly Carole looked in his direction.

"What is it?" Frank said.

"I thought I heard footsteps outside the door."

"Let's find out." Frank moved quickly to the door and yanked it open revealing an empty hallway.

Harper stood still.

"Nothing, sweetheart. It looks like we are both a little on edge."

Shutting the door, he took Carole in his arms. "We're alright now." He began sensuously kissing her neck, his hands caressing her.

"No, Frank, no."

"Yes, oh yes," he mimicked.

Abruptly she pushed him away. "Are we, Frank?"

"What?" Startled by the sudden change Frank shook his head. "Are we what?"

"Alright. You said we were alright now; but we're not. I can't go skulking around like this anymore."

"We've talked about this already. He isn't here is he? He won't be back for ages." Moving to her, Frank gently caressed her shoulders and kissed her cheek.

Oh, to give in, to let him take her now. She let out a deep breath. "Oh, baby."

Harper stepped forward. "Please, I really need your help."

Nothing. No recognition, no sudden looks or turns. To them he didn't exist. "For God's sake, you've got to listen to me."

Caressing Carole, running his hands over her he whispered in her ear. "You know I can't be without you."

Nodding, "I know darling," she whispered softly, letting him fondle her. "Everything could be so good except for one thing."

"I don't have much of job."

"No," she turned away from him. "That's not it. I've got the money and the brains and you've got, well, other talents. It's him. Like I said, I don't want to go skulking around forever."

"Maybe we'll get lucky and he'll drown. He's always in the pool."

"Don't be stupid." She moved into the kitchen and

switched on the kettle. "Frank, tell me you are as trapped as I am."

Weary, and still aching from the accident, Harper sank into a plush white leather settee and closed his eyes. If I could make them listen somehow.

The kettle switched off as Carole lit a cigarette and inhaled deeply.

"You know I want to be with you baby," Frank smiled. "Why don't you just leave him?" he stroked her thighs. "Then we'll get a place of our own and we'll be happy. We won't have to hide from anyone."

"We'll have nothing," she stubbed out her cigarette. 'You can't support me and I haven't worked in years and am not planning on starting now. Anyway, we've talked about this."

Putting his arm around her Frank gently pushed her towards the bedroom. "We'll talk about it later."

Carolee stood still for a moment, avoiding his advances then she sighed. "Alright, but we'll have some music this time." Just before then entered the bedroom, Carolee stopped and took Frank's hand. "This isn't over you know?"

The door closed, drowning Frank's reply.

Harper laid his head on the back of the settee.

A moment later the strains of Barry Manilow floated from the bedroom, mingling with their laughter. The gentle

121

music soothed Harper's pain and he closed his eyes, passing out.

Harper woke suddenly.

Carole's voice was loud over the music. "Of course it's worth it! What are we going to have if we don't do it? I can't get a job, darling, I've no experience at anything. I went from school straight into marriage. I've never worked. Do you seriously think I could start now? And besides I don't want to!"

Frank's reply floated from the now open bedroom door. "Alright, alright. Calm down."

"Let's face it Frank. That's why he is our future. Don't you see? We could have it all. The flat, the money, everything. The sooner it's done, the better."

Harper listened intently, suppressing the panic so near the surface. If he let his concentration slip the fear would grip him. What was happening to him was too difficult to comprehend. That he was invisible to everyone was beyond his understanding.

Frank's voice cut into Harper's thoughts. "Me? Why me all of a sudden?"

There was silence between them, then suddenly Frank appeared from the bedroom nude clutching his jeans. "I thought it was supposed to be us?"

Carole followed tying her robe around her. She pressed her body into Frank's. "It is us, darling, but I'm not big enough or strong enough like you. You know how I couldn't do the whole thing myself."

"Sure, I'm your slave. I do all the dirty work and I'm the one that gets caught."

"Nothing will happen, darling," she whispered, gently kissing him on his forehead, then slowly running her tongue down his cheek planting little caresses over his skin. She bent down, "Hello", she said playfully, her face inches away from the top of his thighs.

He cupped her face, exhaling loudly, and slowly lowered himself with her to the kitchen floor out of sight from Harper. Her tone changed, "then we will have each other and all the money we could dream of."

On the settee, Harper was stunned, suddenly realizing what the two plotters were up to. "You're going to kill him."

Noticing the phone on the table beside the settee, Harper grabbed it, bringing the earpiece to his ear. A strange, eerie, babbling squeal emanated from it. He threw it down just as the music from the bedroom stopped.

From the kitchen the sound of the lovers drove him down the hall to the bathroom.

Facing the mirror he suddenly screamed. Nothing. No reflection, no frightened, bruised face, stared back at him. The mirror was empty.

"It can't be!"

Slapping his cheeks for reassurance he looked again. Still there was no reflection in the mirror.

Closing his eyes he began breathing deeply as panic grew. "Calm down! Calm down! There's a rational explanation. I'm dreaming. That's all it is. A dream. Cold water. Cold water will wake me up. That's it." The dream would end with a slap of water that would wake him. He switched on the cold water tap. Nothing came out. No water, nothing. Deeply afraid, he tried the hot water tap, then the shower taps and the bath taps. Not a single drop of water fell from any of them.

Now terror gripped him like a vice. He staggered out of the bathroom back down the hall to the living room.

"The TV!"

Switching it on, he stood anxiously waiting for it to work; but it remained dead and silent. Cranking the volume on the stereo he got the same result.

"My mobile!" He remembered his mobile phone was in his pocket; but all that came out of it when he switched it on was a howling screech. Would nothing wake him?

What's happening? Oh God, What's happening to me? Please God, help me! He fell onto the comfort of the settee. It's a dream, it has to be a dream. I'm going to wake up now. I've got to wake up!

The front door opened suddenly and Harper jumped up as a large heavyset, jovial man entered wearing a bright, multi-coloured shirt with cream shorts. He walked down the hallway to the bathroom calling out. "Hello! I'm back. Want to go for a swim with me Moosh?"

The toilet flushed.

In the kitchen Frank and Carole sprang apart and Frank quickly pulled on his jeans. They both ducked down behind the counter.

The man came out of the bathroom with a towel draped over his shoulders clutching swimming trunks. It was Carole's husband, Max. He headed into the bedroom.

Harper stared after him, wondering what to do next.

A moment later Max emerged from the bedroom, the shorts replaced by his swimming trunks. "Moosh?" he called, moving into the living room. Getting no response, Max fell heavily onto the settee picked up the remote and switched on the TV.

The screen came to life.

Whirling around, Harper stared at it, then turned back to Max confused and frightened. Why did it work for him and not for me?

Harper heard a faint soft noise from the kitchen as if a drawer was being opened. Ignoring it he deliberately sat down on the coffee table directly in front of Max hoping to block his view. To no avail. All Max saw was his football match on TV, not Harper. As with the others, Harper just did not exist for Max.

"I've got to make you hear me or see me. Your life is in danger!"

Exasperated, Harper jumped up. "I've got to make you understand!"

No reaction.

"I know," and he slowly reached out, touching the other man's cheek. Max simply brushed his face as if scratching an annoying itch, keeping his eyes on the TV.

"I can't even touch you!"

Movement suddenly caught Harper's eye. Looking up, he saw Frank standing behind Max.

Too late, Max turned, hearing Frank behind him. In a great sweeping motion, Frank brought the knife down, chopping at Max once, twice, three times.

The bloody knife dropped onto the carpet as Frank stepped back, staring horrified at the mess. The blood spurting from Max's throat and chest gurgled like a stream over rocks as he rolled off the settee onto the pristine carpet.

"Oh God, what have you done?" Carole screamed from behind Frank, staring at the blood.

"I've done what you wanted me to do."

Vigorously she shook her head. "No!"

"What are you talking about? This is what we

planned."

"I didn't think you would actually go through with it," Carole screamed.

"Yes you did."

"No, I didn't. I was just dreaming. In my mind, Oh God, the mess!" In near hysteria she backed away from Frank.

Grabbing her shoulders, he spoke evenly. "Listen to me. It's what we both want. We are free now. Do you understand? It's over. We are free Carole."

Suddenly the knife slashed through the air as Max in one final effort plunged it deep into Frank's back then fell to the floor. Staggering forward Frank reached for Carole before falling onto the floor near Max.

The blood from both men seeped into the beige carpet, staining the expensive material.

The sudden beeping of the phone off the hook cut through the stillness. Hanging where Harper had dropped it, the tones were normal now; not the babble it had been earlier.

Slowly, he picked it up and put it back in its cradle.

A blood-curdling wail filled the room as Carole screamed in terror. To her, the phone had returned to the cradle by itself. Realizing what she had seen, Harper cried out. "You can see me, can't you?"

Carole pressed herself against the wall, looking

wildly around the room. "Who's there?" she shouted.

"So you can only hear me," he said, moving towards her. "Listen, I saw the whole thing…."
Before he could finish, Carole screamed and suddenly ran past him to the front door, throwing it open, she tore down to landing at the top of the staircase followed by Harper.

"Listen to me! Stop!"

Harper reached out to grab her.

Touching her, she turned in terror, lost her footing and began to fall. In the split second when she seemed to hang in mid-air she saw him completely and then tumbled down the stone stairs rolling into a crumpled heap at the bottom.

Slowly Harper moved down the stairs towards her. From the awkward tilt of her neck and her eyes vacantly staring up at the ceiling, he could see she was dead.

Harper stood still. "The Phone!" It was working a moment ago. He dashed back up the stairs, along the hallway and into the flat straight to the phone. Grabbing it he started dialling. Glancing over at the two dead bodies he dropped the phone in utter terror.

The bodies had disappeared

Harper blinked. The bicycle wheel was turning very slowly now. Lying on the road, bloody and hurt, Harper concentrated on the turning wheel. But it was gradually blurring, getting darker.

Max and Carolee knelt beside him, both perfectly fine.

"God, I didn't see him. He just came out of nowhere," Max said agitated. Gently rubbing Harper's forehead, Carolee soothed, "Frank's just calling an ambulance on his mobile. Just lie still."

Muttering, Max stood up, looking around. "I just didn't see him. I came out of the drive and he came flying around the corner."

Carole gently stroked Harper's hand as a small crowd gathered. Frank, who had been standing a few feet away on his mobile, returned. "I called the ambulance," he said. "But who knows how long they'll be."

Somebody wondered if anyone knew Harper. No one did.

His vision was blurring. If only he could concentrate.

"Where the hell is that ambulance?" cried Max.

As the bicycle wheel made its last few turns, Harper, with a major effort raised his arm.

"I think he wants you, Max," Frank said quietly.

Kneeling, Max took Harper's ice-cold hand. "What is it?"

Licking his dry lips, Harper whispered. "They're going to kill you." The bicycle wheel stopped turning and

Harper died.

The Man With No Face

Sometimes he could just cry.

The sounds and smells of the pub still lingered as Charles Kendall drove home through Epping Forest. Depressed and tired he felt his life had become a dark chasm of boredom and predictability.

Suddenly, a figure loomed out of the darkness. Kendall heard a loud thud as the man fell across the bonnet and hit the windscreen. For a brief moment before the man rolled off the car, Kendall saw he had no face!

Tires screeched on the wet pavement as Kendall hit the brakes. The car slewed sideways, hit the grassy verge and stopped, hard snapping Kendall against the shoulder belt. Stunned, he slowly pushed open the door, climbed out and froze. Where there should have been an injured man there was only empty road.

"What the...?"

Anxious, he began scouring the area; but no matter how hard he searched he saw no sign of blood or any disturbance except for his tire marks on the wet pavement.

The man with no face had gone. His keys fumbled in his shaking fingers as he unlocked the door. As he climbed the stairs to his flat he realised he needed a drink to calm his nerves and went straight to the kitchen completely ignoring his wife Helen. She stood at the sink staring at him wordlessly as he poured himself a generous amount of red wine and drank it. The liquid flowed down his throat, soothing him. God, that feels good, he thought.

"Hello, to you to," Helen said.

Charles looked up suddenly, "What?"

"I do expect at least a hello. Even Pete rates a greeting of some kind."

"Oh, very funny!"

Peter, their unemployed lodger, grinned from the kitchen table. Kendall poured another. "You won't believe what happened tonight."

"What?" she said disinterested. He sat down heavily opposite Traynor and looked at his wife.

"I was driving along manor road, like always; But just as I came over the little rise, this man stepped out in front of me. He had no face."

Peter's eyebrows went up. "No face? I think you're getting a little paranoid, Charlie."

Charles took another gulp. "No, you don't understand. I mean he had no face. Just a flat expanse of skin. No nose no mouth, no eyes, nothing."

Helen touched his shoulder. "You must have been dreaming while you were driving. Remember your 40th when I was so tired I was still sitting and talking but making no sense because I was really asleep?"

"Helen, I hit this man. He rolled right up on the bonnet and his face, or what should have been his face, was right there in front of me."

She stared at him. "You hit him!"

He nodded, thinking how cold her touch was. "I thought so but when I got out to check, he was gone. No trace of him. So now I'm not so sure."

"Gone?"

Nodding, he watched her sit down. "Honey, go get out of your suit into your jim-jams and I'll put the kettle on."

Slowly it dawned on him that she didn't believe him.

"It was probably a burglar wearing a mask," said Peter dropping his empty beer bottle into the rubbish bin.

Kendall, glared at him. "Right! Get your coats. Both of you!"

"Darling this is not necessary."

"Yes it is," Kendall said, leading them out of the flat.

The car slowly rolled to a stop a few yards from where Kendall had first seen the man with no face. He switched off the engine pointing across the road. "There."

"Honey, there's nothing there but trees."

Climbing out of the car Kendall turned his collar up against the rain, slammed the door and ran quickly across the road. He glanced back at Helen and Peter who followed him resignedly.

"It's nothing but wet grass." Helen said.

"No it isn't." Kendall triumphantly pointed to tire tracks that cut a swathe through the rough grass. "Those tracks prove it," he grinned, vindicated.

"It doesn't prove anything except that a car went off the road here." Peter looked at Charles, then at Helen. "Well don't you think so?"

"These are recent tracks. Hardly anybody uses this road so the chance of somebody else going off the road in so short a space of time is remote. It proves it." He marched back to the car full of satisfaction. He knew those tire marks were his. They just had to be.

Behind him, Peter called out, "You're jumping to all kinds of conclusions, Charlie."
"You didn't see his face so it doesn't matter. Let it go."

Ignoring the irritation in Helen's voice, he shook his head. "No, I'm going to phone the police. If I don't it's all going to fall on top of me!"

"Do you really think everything's going to be okay if you do phone the police?"

They drove home in silence.

Charlie moved into the kitchen, picked up the phone and sat down at the table. Catching Helen's angry look he stared back defiantly. "Helen, it has to be reported. The man was hurt because I ran him over. It's the only way to cover myself!"

"There was absolutely no proof out there that you hit anybody," Peter stood up, looking at Kendall.

"He could identify my car. I'm not taking any chances." Kendall growled at the lodger.

"How could he identify anything with no face?"

"That's it!" Helen shouted. "I'll phone the police!" Grabbing the phone from Kendall she pushed him away and suddenly he realised how upset she was. His own frustration deflated as he sat down. Was he over the top? The consequences of not reporting it would have been far worse. He must report it first before the police find the injured man in a hospital near by.

Suddenly, the phone slammed down. Charlie started as Helen turned to him. "You just get so ridiculous sometimes! Why couldn't you just leave it alone?"

"I don't believe this! What exactly are you trying to say, Inspector?" Kendall watched the Inspector, a tall, lean, tired looking man, turn from the window. How he wished he had never run over the man. He would've been in his bed now. "It's very late Mr Kendall and I am trying to make sense of what you've told me."

"Well, question the rest of the neighbours on this street if you don't believe me!"

Tired, Kendall watched the Inspector pull a little red

notebook from his pocket, and a ring binder. "We are, but we've drawn a blank so far." He flipped open the notebook. "Just for the record, I'd like to make sure I have the details right."

Kendal studied the Inspector, clenching his fists in frustrations at the big man's slowness. He was about to erupt when suddenly the Inspector looked up.

"You stated you were driving along Manor Road. It was dark, wet and cold. You saw a figure ahead and when he came into your headlights you hit the man and as he rolled onto the bonnet you saw he had no face. That right?"

Kendal moved to the fireplace and absently picked up a small framed photo of his wife, "I'm not sure if I did hit him," he said, turning the photo over and over.

"Either you hit the man or you didn't. Which is it?"

Suddenly, Kendall slammed the picture onto the mantle piece. Bits of glass fell onto the carpet. "Look. I saw the man just as he stepped out in front of me. I stopped the car, got out and looked around, but there was no sign of him. I told you I checked the area, came home and called you. I have done my duty."

Kendall glanced at his wife, who stifled a yawn. Is it too much for you, he thought? Bored are we? I'm fighting for my life and you're just sitting there, disinterested. She crossed her legs as elegantly as she could in her old pink robe. He looked away in disgust. An iceberg.

"I hope you're not wasting my time, Mr Kendall. Do you have any witnesses?"

"Of course not!" he snorted, shoving his hands in his pockets nervously. "Look it was probably a burglar wearing a mask." He picked up one of Helen's little glass figurines. Part of the collection that filled every spare narrow space in the house. "Check the hospitals!" He waved his hand. "Check the woods! He should be easy to find."

Kendall shivered and quickly looked away from the Inspector's cold, unblinking, gaze.

"Why didn't you look in the woods for him yourself Mr Kendall?"

He glanced back as the Inspector closed his notebook. "I told you! I stopped. I got out and searched along the road, and in the immediate woods. For him to get so far away in so short a time he would've been running, which must be what happened because he was gone."

They looked at each other, silently assessing. Kendall could feel the man's gaze burning into him. He felt sure he knew what the policeman was thinking. Was he guilty or was he innocent? Was it the truth or a pack of lies? They stared at each other for a moment. The Inspector seemed to be about to say something, about to move. Here it comes, Kendall thought, the handcuffs, the long court case.

The Inspector yawned. "Thank you for your time, Mr Kendall. I'll be in touch soon." Picking up his hat, he moved towards the door, stopping by Helen. He nodded, wearily. "Good evening, er, morning, Mrs Kendal."

Charles turned away and let out a loud sigh. How close that had been. A wave of relief flooded over him. Staring down at the figurine in his hand he did not see the long look between his wife and the Inspector. He only heard the door close softly behind him.

Two days of rain. Kendall hoped the tracks hadn't been washed away as he searched through the mud and grass beside the road. His shoes soaked through. According to the police no body had yet been found. That left him trying to find something that would prove the man had run off after the accident, not badly hurt at all. If he could do that then he could not be charged with hit and run. Technically, he had reported the accident but only several hours after it occurred and he didn't stay at the scene. It was all so worrying.

Twigs snapped, tall grass squelched against his legs, the cold water soaking through to the skin. Suddenly water filled his shoe as mud squelched up to his knee.

"Damn!"

As the slime oozed up his trousers, he realised how foolish he must look. Gingerly, he pulled his leg out of the

138

mud and watched it drip off his shoe. He sighed heavily.
Perhaps, Helen was right, he had been dreaming while he
was driving. He knew his wife had been so tired at his 40th
birthday party that she had fallen asleep while talking to
one of the last guests.

Perhaps the same thing happened to him. He must
have imagined the whole thing. Only an idiot would go this
far, he thought.

Turning back towards the car, he suddenly stopped.
A dark, crimson patch of cloth just under a small bush a
few feet ahead caught his eye. It was not part of the
underbrush and he squelched towards it, his excitement
building.

Triumphantly, Charlie entered the dark flat, closing the door
noisily he climbed the stairs two at a time. It was past
midnight. He didn't notice Helen's clothes strewn recklessly
across the floor, dropped as if in a hurry to get in bed. He
didn't notice the overly heavy scent of her perfume that
masked the smells of the pub. It didn't dawn on him that
she had only just come in. He felt sure Helen would want
to share in his triumph.

That night he tossed and turned, the blurred faces and
bodies seemed to be everywhere. Each time he turned
they were there; closer than before. Their voices were

insistent, loud but still incomprehensible. He woke suddenly, full of the disjointed uneasiness of a nightmare.

Later in the morning as the dawn's light trickled through the windows the Inspector arrived unexpectedly. Kendall watched Helen smile at him as he entered. "Would you like some tea, Inspector?"

Kendall stepped forward as they sat down his hands behind his back. "Why do I have the pleasure of your visit so very early in the morning?"

"I just wanted to get one or two things cleared up in my mind."

"The last time you were here, Inspector, you didn't believe a word I said. You probably haven't even bothered to pursue any line of inquiry have you?"

"On the contrary, we've been investigating this case very vigorously. I believe we are on the verge of a breakthrough."

K   endall watched him smile at Helen as she brought the tea. Was it a little too bright, a little too long? Or was he just imagining it.

"A breakthrough! That's good." Helen said pleasantly, pouring milk into the man's mug.

"Yes it is."

Charles watched the Inspector slowly sip his tea, his irritation rising at the plodding slowness of the detective. Finally, unable to contain himself, Kendall cried out. "I can give you a breakthrough you weren't expecting."

"Oh, and how is that sir?"

"This!" From his back pocket Kendall produced a piece of torn and jagged crimson cloth. "The very evidence that proves I saw a man out there and that he ran away after the accident. I couldn't possibly have found him, therefore I'm in the clear."

Gingerly, the Inspector put his tea down and stood up taking the material from Kendal. "Well, this is very interesting indeed. We found a man's jacket just like this about ten feet from the road." The Inspector moved a step closer to Kendall. "My guess is, Mr Kendall, the lab will prove that this cloth matches the jacket and," he paused looking at them both, "the fibres we found on the front of your car."

"My car?" Kendall stared, stunned. "But I checked the car. It was clean."

"Not quite. There were some things you missed."

"It doesn't matter. This cloth proves the man ran away from the scene after the accident occurred. I reported the accident as soon as I got home. That cloth is my proof!"

"What cloth?"

Horror-struck, Kendall watched the Inspector pick up the box of matches from the mantle, strike a match and light the cloth. As it burned he dropped it into the grate and looked up at Kendal. "You were saying something about a cloth?"

Kendall looked on incredulously. "What's going on here? You can't do this!"

Kendall moved towards the fireplace only to be pushed back the Inspector. "Yes I can. There's enough evidence on your car alone to put you away for a long time."

"My car? My car is clean, I checked it myself. Just a dent that's all." Panic began to overwhelm him. The Inspector smiled slightly. "Thanks to Helen we were able to find blood and fibres on the right side light and front grill both of which were shattered by the impact."

Kendall glared at her. "What have you done?"

Shrugging, Helen stood up and moved to the Inspector. "Jack helped me make sure the evidence was suitably convincing."

Dumbstruck, Charlie looked at the two. "Jack? Helen? What the hell..."

The Inspector put his arm around her. "We met last year when you were burgled, ever since then we've been together off and on. Grabbing what time we could before you came home or before I went on duty."

Taking the Inspector's hand, Helen sat down and smiled at Charlie. "Jack just added bits of fibre and blood to make the evidence more convincing. It was all really very easy."

Feeling sick, Kendall stared at his wife. He couldn't believe she would be that devious. Nausea filled his stomach as disbelief swept over him. Nearly fainting, he caught sight of something shiny in the Inspector's hands and realised with horror it was his pair of handcuffs. Stunned, Kendal's arm was pulled behind him as the first cuff clamped tightly over his wrist.

"You see, Mr Kendall, none of this would've happened if we hadn't had an accident the night before. Helen was going to leave you; but suddenly we were in a precarious position."

He stared at the Inspector, unable to speak, numbed from shock. Watching the big man's lips work Kendall barely heard the words. "...a chance to get you out of the way and avoid prison." He smiled coldly. "You see, we accidently ran over the same man the night before. We had to do something so we set it up for the next night. I tied a rope around him and waited for you to come along. You always take that road approximately the same time every evening. It wasn't hard to work out. As soon as you hit him I hauled back into the woods."

Kendall's throat was dry. He tried to speak but nothing came out. He felt cold metal clamp over his other wrist while the Inspector continued. "If you'd looked harder you would have found us; but you didn't spend more than

15 minutes there. You drove away from an accident scene. That's hit and run, Mr Kendall. The punishment is prison. The fact that you ran over a man we accidently killed won't make any difference. Everything points to you."

The Inspector's big hands pushed Kendall in the back as he stumbled forward, through the hallway to the waiting police car outside, tears streaming down his face as he stumbled forward.

Kendall lay in the bed unmoving. A needle, filled with drugs was pushed into his arm by a young, efficient and quite pretty nurse. She did not look at him. The green liquid quickly disappeared into his arm as the needle was emptied. Kendall's eyes moved around looking at the two men, dressed entirely in black standing at the foot of the bed. The one called Davis spoke to the older, balding man standing beside him.

"So Cain, what now?"

"We keep going, break him down until there is nothing left."

"Well there won't be much left. He thinks his wife has left him, he's going to jail for a murder he didn't commit. What more do we throw at him."

Cain stared at Davis. "You know the drill. We feed him enough images to break down his resistance and then we fill him with the images we want him to see, hear and feel."

Davis snorted. "Right so all his preconceptions are gone."

"If you're uncomfortable with this Davis then you'd better find another position within the Agency."

"I just think that we could do it a different way. We're asking them to kill for Queen and country. Do we really need to rip their minds apart?"

Cain, picked up the chart hanging on the end of the bed and looked at it. Then he glanced up at Davis. "It's the only way. You know that."

"And just how many successes has your pet project had? Two? Out of more than ten subjects? Face it Cain, your project is a failure. I'm going for a fag."

Cain watched Davis leave the room and then he looked down into Kendall's eyes. He saw fear in them, fear that he had put there. Turning to the nurse he said, "up the dosage." Kendall's eyes widened as the fear turned to terror. Cain smiled. "Make the dosage the highest yet. I have a feeling this one will be number three."

With that Cain left the room feeling very good about the project. Yes, this one would be number three.

In his bed, paralyzed save for his eyes, Kendall wanted to scream.

The Pilot

Herbert Petrie blinked.

He stared at the plastic model airplane on the workbench in front of him. He could still feel the engine's vibrations, the fierce slipstream rushing by the open canopy. What a dream that was!

He knew he was not rising up from an English airbase in a fully armed fighter heading for the French coast to blast German targets. Herbert hadn't been alive during the war. He'd never been near an aircraft. He was afraid of heights!

Yet the dream had been so real. By reading everything he could on aircraft and flying he felt he could fly, if only he had the strength to do it. The surroundings were back in focus now. Shelves displaying various types of completed model planes lined three walls of the cramped loft workroom. Along the fourth wall was his workbench with the latest addition, a stubby, powerful British fighter, the Hawker Typhoon, in a cleared space on the crowded workbench. Hours and hours spent on this masterpiece had created a true, detailed replica of the aircraft in miniature.

"Herbert!" A harsh voice suddenly broke his reverie.

"Herbert! It's almost dark and you still haven't cut the grass or taken out the rubbish!"

His wife, Linda. She was upset because he escaped to his workroom to daydream.

She's right, he thought, I've ignored my work and come up here to play. I must be more responsible, but....

He glanced lovingly at his new masterpiece, then sighed, shut off the light, closed the door, locking it. Turning away he thought he heard the faint sounds of aircraft diving and rolling, guns chattering as they flew, but the sounds abruptly faded away. Overactive imagination, he thought.

Later on, as darkness fell, Herbert, a quiet little man, finished cutting the grass, took out the rubbish and washed the kitchen floor while listening to Linda complain about being cooped up in the house all day. He longed for his little room in the loft.

Tired and sleepy, he carefully readied himself for bed. At her dressing table, Linda brushed her long, blonde hair, watching him in the mirror. "Herbert, you've got to talk to your boss about a rise."

"They aren't giving out rises any more."

Exasperated, she banged down her brush. "What about Jim? He just got a rise and a promotion."

"There was just one position and he was the logical one to fill it."

"But you've been there eight years!"

She watched him methodically pull back the duvet,

smooth out the under sheet and climb into bed. What a plodder, she thought. Sometimes she just wanted to scream at him but after nine years the twinkle in his eye still made her heart flutter. Why couldn't he be more aggressive?

"Darling, if you want something you've got to go after it. Everybody has more than we do and I want my share!"

"We must go carefully. Times are tough these days and I can't afford to rock the boat."

"You've never rocked the boat and you never will!" Slamming her make-up drawer, she angrily turned out the light and fell heavily into bed. How could she let herself get so angry? She was more upset with herself for letting his carefulness get to her.

After a moment, she reached out and squeezed his hand. "I'm sorry, darling," she whispered.

"Me too," he said, gently squeezing back. He'd never be a mover it just wasn't in him. Talking to his boss about a rise gave him stomach cramps. Shutting off the bedside lamp, he rolled over and dreamed of airplanes.

The cold grey water of the Channel shot by under his wing. Four hundred miles an hour! Coming in under radar, the Germans were about to get a rude awakening. Fully armed, the four cannon and eight rockets would make a mess of the target, a German railyard a few miles inland from the French coast.

Throttles open wide, the engine roared its approval as the beach shot by under his wing a few seconds later. He thumbed off the safety catch, banking the fighter towards the target.

"Petrie!"

Startled, Herbert looked up to see his boss standing over him. "What's wrong with you, Herbie?"

"Nothing," the little man murmured. He really disliked Herbie.

"Good!"

Herbert wished his boss, Daniel R. Gidney, a large, heavyset forceful, man would go away. Instead he dropped a thick folder on his desk that Herbert knew only too well.

"Herbie, this report needs more work. I can't present it at tomorrow's meeting; the sales projections for next year just aren't good enough. Next year's budget has to be higher than this years, not the same!"

"The figures reflect the times. They are realistic."

"Realistic?" Sitting on the edge of the desk, Gidney began to poke Herbert in the shoulder. "Listen Herbie, we've got to prove this division is moving ahead, making money. The board wants a successful firm. Otherwise we'll be forced to cut back and people will lose their jobs. Do you want that, Herbert?"

He shook his head as Gidney stood up.

"Good, let's hop to it then."

"It'll be on your desk first thing."

"No, no, no!" cried Gidney. "I need it tonight! I've got to prepare for the meeting. Thanks to you my dinner engagement will be ruined unless you get it to the house early, before dark. I might just make desert then. Don't be late. I don't want to be up all night."

Before Herbert could answer Gidney turned away, disappearing into his plush office.

Sighing, Herbert glanced around his tiny cubicle crowded with a desk, computer, filing cabinet and another chair, like everybody else's. Except Gidney's. He reached for the phone to call his wife. It was going to be another long night.

The great cylinders pounding out thousands of horsepower sent shivers through him. Every nerve tingled, adrenalin pumping through his veins as the fighter raced over hills, fields and rivers. Grinning from ear to ear, he whooped with glee. The anticipation of battle tensed every muscle, pumping his heart faster as the target came into view. A long German troop train was pulling out of the siding.

Now, the locomotive was in his gun sight. Thumbing the firing button on the control stick, the four cannon exploded into life, spitting fire. The steam engine erupted into sheets of flame under the hammering of his shells. The force of the blows on the locomotive derailed it bringing it to a sudden, grinding halt while behind the goods wagons began to pile into each other. Banking sharply, he brought the fighter around and attacked again watching his shells stitch a pattern of destruction the length of the train. Now, what was left of the locomotive belched smoke as the wagons snaked and twisted jumping the tracks and smashing into each other. Pulling the stick back, he put the fighter into a tight climbing turn away from the carnage below. Time for the next target.

Herbert blinked. Sweat rolled down his body as he gripped the steering wheel. God that had been so real. Smoke still lingered in his nostrils, the hammering cannon still in his ears and the roaring engine still sending vibrations through him.

Fear began to stir the edges of his mind, mixed with curiosity. If he could somehow control.... The sensations quickly died away as he realised he was sitting in Gidney's driveway. The lights on the huge, fairy tale house gleamed in the twilight. Built of red brick it had white shutters on all the windows and a long porch protected the polished, oak front doors while the sloping roof was supported by ornate pillars, regularly spaced along its length.

The door opened suddenly. "It's about time," Gidney shouted, moving rapidly down the steps to the car. "Where's that report, Herbie?"

"Here," Herbert said softly, passing it through the open window.

Grabbing it, Gidney growled. "My dinner appointment was for eight and now it's nine-thirty. Probably served dessert already. Had to have cold leftovers tonight. I'm going to have heartburn because of you tomorrow, Herbie. These figures better be good." Turning suddenly, Gidney marched back into his house and slammed the door.

Herbert headed for home.

"Your dinner is cold," Linda said flatly. She sat on the settee, watching a television that displayed only orange and purple pictures as he came in.

Nodding, he went straight to the bedroom and began to change. Carefully, folding his trousers he laid them on the bed, brushed the lint off them, straightened the material to make sure the crease was just right before hanging them up. Linda appeared in the doorway.

"I want a new flatscreen TV."

"We can't afford it right now."

"Herbert, we've got money in the bank so we're getting one as well as one of those new Sky boxes. I've been waiting too long for you to replace that piece of shit!"

She stared at him, waiting for his reply. A little man in his underwear, balding, approaching middle age with a spare tire round his belly. When they were first married he was larger than life, quick-witted, intelligent, his expressive eyes filled with laughter. Now she saw an ambitionless man. The laughter was still there and he still moved her but she wished he was more passionate. She wanted to shout at him to wake up, live life, and be spontaneous.

"It's time we moved ahead and joined the human race, dear. I'm going out to work and we'll put this dump up for sale. My sister has a new car, new furniture, new TV and a big new house. I want the same things Herbert."

"Sweetie, the house is almost paid for. Be patient."

"No! I'm getting too old to be patient!" Marching back downstairs to the living room, she fell heavily onto the old settee in front of the two-tone television. Patient, how many times had she heard that? "I'm getting a new TV tomorrow and that's final."

Later as Linda slept, Herbert went up to his workroom. As he unlocked the door he heard sounds of aircraft diving and rolling in desperate dogfights. They abruptly disappeared as soon as he opened the door.
He looked at his models, static, unmoving where he had left them, where they had always been. Yet... Didn't they

look slightly different somehow? Must be imagining things. Sitting down, he lovingly, tenderly picked up the completed Typhoon, turning it over and over, feeling the power in his hands, the sound of the engine. He wished.

The German plane shot over him. Flames licked along the Typhoon's nose. Quickly kicking the rudder he pushed the stick forward, diving the fighter, the pulverising slipstream hammering out the fire.

Ramming the throttle into maximum he dove after the enemy plane. The German turned sharply, forcing him to overshoot. Shells thudded into his aircraft. Yanking the stick back hard he pulled the fighter into a tight loop and the German shot underneath. Levelling out, Herbert banked sharply, fired and watched the enemy fighter explode into a burning fireball.

"Herbie! Herbie!"

Everything came back into focus - the office, his cubicle, everybody staring at him and Gidney, red-faced, standing over him.

"Have you gone deaf, Petrie?" Gidney slapped the report on his desk. Herbert hoped he would never see it again, but there it was. He stared at it.

"Do you know what happened in the meeting," Gidney shouted? Before Herbert could answer, the big man continued. "I'll tell you what happened. The board was not pleased. There was talk of cutbacks in management. Cutbacks in management Petrie! Fingers were pointed at this department, in my direction. They said the figures weren't good enough."

"They were accurate. That's what you asked for."

"Accurate? Can't you understand simple English? I wanted you to prove to the board that we were out of the recession, like all the other divisions, making a profit!"

"That would be lying."

"Lying!" Incredulous, Gidney stared around the room at the others watching silently. "Did you hear that? He said that would be lying." Suddenly, Gidney shoved his face inches from Herbert's. The booze on his breath as ugly as the broken veins in his nose.

"Do you know what imagination is Herbie?"

He hated Herbie.

"Have you ever heard of creativity? That's what I wanted. Some creativity, some imagination. All you gave me was accurate!" Gidney screamed.

Herbert couldn't answer. He had arguments that would wilt Gidney, bowl him over, but they stuck in his throat, at the back of his tongue, locked away by fear. Instead he just stared at his computer, feeling very small.

Gidney shouted again. "We need people with creativity, here, not tombstones! The board wants cutbacks; well the first cutback starts with you! Clean out your desk and get out!" Gidney stalked back into his office and slammed the door.

Stunned, driving home, he didn't see his driveway. Shock and hurt began to give way to rage and frustration.

Linda was in bed with one of her migraines, a wet washcloth over her head. She knew the source of her headache. Herbert. She was always pushing him. If the house was burning down he'd still be in his workroom with his ridiculous models. Well, that too, was going to change.

The front door suddenly crashed open.

In spite of the pain she sat up, heard his footsteps run up the stairs and the workroom door open and slam shut. It was too early for him to be home. Something was wrong. The pain was awful but she had to get up for both their sakes. She had to take charge yet again.

Leaning against the closed door, Herbert calmed himself then slowly approached the bench. Would it work? Carefully sitting down, he tenderly ran his fingers over the Typhoon. "I wish, I wish...." Soon the roaring engine drowned his wife's calls out. He closed his eyes.

Water skimmed underneath as he dropped to wave level as the shoreline appeared in his sights. He still had plenty of ammunition. The cannon were only half full and the rockets hadn't been used. Banking sharply, he climbed over buildings, heading towards the Essex countryside as the sun was setting. The beautiful fairytale house came into view and a devilish grin creased his face. "I hate Herbie," he shouted. "Do you hear me Gidney? I hate Herbie!"

His cannon burst into life spitting fire. Fingering another button on the control stick there was a sudden loud whoosh as all eight of the rockets fell from their moorings under the wings and shot towards the house. Within seconds, Gidney's stately, house was engulfed in an orange fireball, the flames reaching hundreds of feet into the air.

Herbert circled the wreckage, smiling, then turned and climbed away.

Witnesses, four teenagers drinking beer in their yard, said the house had been destroyed from the sky. No one believed them. No flight had been any where near that vicinity. It would have showed on radar and radar showed nothing. The Gidneys, shocked and stunned, had been out for dinner at the time.

No trace, no clues. Three days seemed like three years without him. Everyday she stood in his workroom, looking at all the models. What did he see in them? What was it that fascinated him so? Perhaps if she could see it too…?

This time something caught her eye. She thought the one on the bench had moved since the last time she came in.Nonsense! It was her grief-stricken mind playing tricks.

She studied the model of the Typhoon realising it was different from the others, somehow real. Almost as if it could fly. Picking it up slowly, sadly, she carefully caressed it and suddenly felt the throb of a roaring engine run through her.

Emerging from heavy cloud into brilliant sunshine, Herbert saw the formation of enemy fighters below him. Suddenly he saw a shape climbing rapidly towards him. The new arrival tucked in beside him, just off his wing and Herbert grinned hugely when he saw the other pilot's long, blonde hair.

A moment later, they wheeled around together heading for the enemy aircraft, the sun behind them.

Thug

Two old Bedford vans thundered by, angry faces peering from every window.

They were still looking for him.

They won't get me, he thought. If only his leg wasn't so badly mashed, he could move deeper into Epping Forest and hide. The road was still only a few hundred feet away. Toby Moore crawled painfully along the ground, towards the iron gate of St Peter's Church. It would be dark soon and he could hide inside. At the gate, Toby pulled himself up. Pain hammered through his blood-soaked leg from the smashed bone. Steeling himself, he hobbled the few feet to the door, falling heavily against it, nearly fainting with pain. Locked.

The Bastards!

He was so weak he couldn't even begin to break it down. Painfully, he moved around the side and glanced up at the stained glass windows. Easy to smash, he thought, a rock, a brick, easy-peasey. I'll show them. Anger suddenly filled him. I'll get them back.

Scooping up a nearby rock, he hurled it at the priceless glass that shattered loudly.
Suddenly, voices cried. A van slammed on its brakes. "The Church!" "Did you hear it? This way!"

Stupid!

He'd forgotten about the patrols. Why couldn't he for once control his temper? The window was too high to climb with his poor leg, so he dragged himself away into the graveyard.

Asif Khan, head of the citizens militia, stood outside the Church, hands on his hips staring at the broken window. He turned to the others. "This little shit hates everything good in this country. Well, we're going to teach him to have some respect."

In the overgrown graveyard, Toby watched from behind a large old tombstone. Some of the men he knew, neighbours in the block of flats he lived in down the street. The same flats he and his gang regularly vandalised. Some were from the houses he burgled opposite the forest, while others were from the surrounding streets in the area. All of them had been terrorized by his gang until now. His victims were no longer cowering behind locked doors. They were armed and hunting him.

"Anybody check the end house?" He heard Asif say.

"Been empty since the old lady died." Teri, a young Frenchman, replied.

The voices filtered up to him. He could see the shotguns and rifles they carried. Shotgun pellets had smashed his leg. He would wait here until dark then head for the old house.

Anger burned in Asif. Standing outside the Church as his men searched inside he thought of how the green peaceful community, his home for 30 years had been blighted by Moore. He thought of the burglaries, the vandalism, the young girl they raped and the old woman Moore had clubbed to death. He could see Toby's sneering face as he stepped out of Snaresbrook Crown Court, free. The witnesses had retracted their statements there was no evidence for any of his crimes. Now justice was in his hands. I intend to make the most of it, he thought.

Since the government had lifted restrictions for 24 hours, allowing local groups to clean up their own streets after a prolonged and violent crime wave, the people of Britain were fighting back. This is just the beginning, he thought. He turned as Norman Strong, the local ironmonger, came out of the woods. "We found a lot of blood by the big oak, so he must be badly wounded."

Asif smiled, "Good, then he can't go very far."

"Look, let's just wait for him here. If he's badly wounded sooner or later he'll need help."

Asif snorted. "Help! Don't forget what this animal has done, Norman. He's getting no help from me!"

Norman, a large, heavy set man, holding his shotgun awkwardly, wiped his sweating forehead. He looked at Asif's sharp features, long nose, piercing fiery eyes. The man is driven, he thought. "The time limit is over.

There's nothing he can do now. He's wounded, his gang is gone. Let's just leave him and go home."

"So it can start all over again? I saw his victims when I worked at the hospital."

"It doesn't matter, Asif. These guns are registered with the police. They know who we are and that we are past the limit. They're going to come after us too!"

Asif spat. "You're too soft, Norman. We get Moore and we go home, that's the plan. Come on."

It won't end just yet, Asif thought as they moved into the Church. There's so much else to do.

Toby stared at the outline of the house in the darkness. Sitting against the tombstone, he stared at it for a long time. Occasionally it disappeared behind branches blown by the wind but he knew it was there. There was hope after all. How far was it? Ten yards or a hundred it made no difference. He could barely move. "Sod you!" he cried. "I'm not dying out here!"

Slowly, he began to crawl, dragging his useless leg along the ground. Much later, he stopped for the last time, tired, weak, out of breath. The house, now only a few feet away was the last one at the end of row of terraced houses. He moved to the kitchen window. Behind him, in the woods he could hear the thrashing feet of his pursuers. Voices cried excitedly for the others to follow. They'd found his trail. A van screeched up on the curb just past the house. Toby ducked. Another van pulled up by the Church. More voices sounded from the woods behind the houses. They were closing in. He looked inside.

Suddenly, the overhead light in the kitchen went on. He ducked again, waiting a few moments then peered over the sill. It was clean and tidy with a gas fire glowing softly in the corner. A pot of something sat on the cooker. Someone had probably bought the place and just moved in. It doesn't matter. This window was much lower than the ones in the Church. He might just be able to climb inside. There was no time to look for another way in.

Trying the window, to his amazement he found it was unlocked. Fools. Just inviting people like me to drop in. Painfully, he hauled himself up over the sill and fell onto the floor. He turned abruptly as the window shut and the light went out.

He lay in the darkness as voices went past the window outside. "What about the house?"

"It's empty. We looked already."

"Check the back gardens. He can't be far away!"

The voices drifted away. Closing his eyes he waited for the light to come on again; but it didn't. Suddenly, he realised the room was cold and damp. The fire no longer glowing. What the hell? Sweat rolled down his face.

"Tohhbeee!" A cold, hissing whisper in the darkness, sent shivers down his spine.

Alarmed he sat up on his elbows. "Who's there?"

A low guttural chuckle answered him, making his blood curdle. Instinct told him he was in grave danger. Pulling himself up he limped around the wall desperately searching for the light switch. Light would make things better. As he stumbled around the horrible, hissing chuckle followed him. His heart pumped faster and faster. The hairs on the back of neck stood up. Where the hell was that switch. Finally, it was in his hands. Relief flooded through him as he turned it on.

No bright light penetrated the darkness. No light to calm his escalating fear. Only the soft, evil laughter filled the room.

"Tohhbee!"

He turned suddenly, his leg collapsing under him as he fell to the floor. Weak and dizzy he pushed himself up, he fell back against the wall and peered into the darkness. Fear now filled every fibre in him. His hands shook, sweat poured down his skin and his throat was dry. "Who are you?" he whispered hoarsely.

"Remember...."

Toby shook his head. The infection in his leg had created a fever and his mind was playing tricks on him. That was the answer. If he could just find a working light switch he would be alright. It was all in his mind, it had to be. Then he saw the movement in the shadows and heard the slinking, slippery sliding of something crawling towards him. "No."

"Remember Tohhbee."

It was getting closer. He licked his dry lips and tried to move but fear held him paralysed. He screwed up his courage. This was a game. "Remember what?" he spat.

"Remember." The evil chuckle raised his fear to terror.

The darker than dark shadow slithered closer to him the soft laughter filling his ears. He tired to scream; but the sound just died in his throat. Suddenly, he saw a glimpse of the face, a twisted rotting face so horrible he nearly choked. But there was something familiar about it, something he knew.

"Remember," it grinned at him.

The old woman he beat to death for trying to stop him robbing her house. The face slithered closer.

"Remember, Toby."

Her features were recognizable in the terrible face. It was the old woman. "No," he cried. He stilled himself, defiant. "Yes," he gulped. "I remember and I'm glad. She got in the way."

Suddenly, the face changed right in front of him, growing more grotesque, more horrible, and with it the stench of rotting flesh filled his nostrils. "Remember, this one," it whispered.

It couldn't be. Mounting nausea filled his throat as sweat poured down his face, his head thumping with fever. Choking, he recognised this face too. "I remember," he croaked.

"Whooo?"

"A girl... Nobody special."

"What did you dooo?"

He gulped, swallowing hard, trying to keep his fear down. Nausea and vomit rushed up his throat. He choked, remembering the drunken orgy after the pub closed. "We just had some fun," he said defiant again.

"What did you do?" the shape insisted slithering closer to him.

"We were drunk. We had a good time. That's all. We got a little carried away," he croaked, the words tumbling out of him. Something bright glinted in the gloom as the shadow suddenly rose over him. The horrific mutilated face grinned and hissed. "You raped her Tohbee! You murdered her Tohbee!"

He remember the girl, how she begged him to stop. They'd been drunk at a party. On the way home he'd forced himself on her again and again. Through her protests he'd said things like, "you were asking for it. You wanted it. You were giving me the eye all night." When she screamed he'd grabbed the biggest rock he could handle and hit her several times.

The shadow slithered around him,the stench of its rotting flesh making him gag. "Remember," it hissed.

"Now you will know what it's like to be a victim."

This time his scream passed his lips in a loud wail as the shadow pounced and tore at him.

Norman came slowly out of the house, took his handkerchief away from his mouth and sucked in some clean air. It had started to rain. The others stood by the vans parked in the road, Asif amongst them. Unsteadily, Norman joined them. "It's Moore alright."

Teri, the young Frenchman, who ran a local bistro slung his shotgun over his shoulder. "What happened?"

Norman shrugged. "That place has broken glass and metal everywhere. Probably crawled through the window and bled to death. His leg wound was very bad. I wouldn't wish that on anyone."

"I would," Asif glanced at the others. "I saw what he did to those people. I'm glad he died that way. Now we go after the lawyers, judges and politicians that always let him and others like him off free then....".

"No!" Teri, shook his head. "It's over."

Nodding, Norman turned away. "Yes, it's over. We've done enough." He wondered if he would ever forget the look of utter terror on Toby's face. "What did he see that made him so afraid?"

Teri shrugged. "Maybe he was afraid of dying?"

"Don't you know?" All eyes turned towards Asif who stared back at them. "That was Mary's old house. The one he beat to death," he said evenly. Then suddenly he grinned. "Who knows? Maybe he saw her."

Printed in Great Britain
by Amazon